BAD BLOOD

Julia McAllister Mysteries Book Three

Marilyn Todd

SAPERE
BOOKS

BAD BLOOD

Published by Sapere Books.

20 Windermere Drive, Leeds, England, LS17 7UZ,
United Kingdom

saperebooks.com

ISBN: 978-1-80055-373-6

To Martin —
friends for so long, I've forgotten which of us is the bad influence.

CHAPTER 1

'Tell me, John,' Julia McAllister said as she slipped into the seat opposite Inspector John Collingwood, blocking his view with the ostrich plumes in her hat. 'Do you believe in reincarnation?'

Collingwood moved his chair sideways. 'Why? Are you worried you were a bloodhound in a previous life, after tracking me to this club?'

'It crossed my mind. Do you know how many I tried?' Never mind how much time she'd wasted that could have been spent searching out models, rekindling contacts, anything to get her foot back through the door of the saucy picture trade. Belts, so help her, were getting tighter by the minute. Another month and they'd start to look like bracelets. 'The reason I'm curious is because I'm going to kill you, if you don't sober up.'

'In which case, I'd be obliged if you could make it quick and clean and painless.'

In this whirlpool of booze and cigar smoke, Julia imagined a man could very happily stretch out in his chair, back to the wall, and tell himself that everything was right with the world. He could drink strong liquor, with or without ice, with or without shaving, and nobody judged. Why would they? How could they? Not while dancers tossed froths of red petticoats over their bottoms, held one leg by the ankle above their heads, and agreed terms for an hour, sometimes less, of affection.

'I appreciate your concern, Julia, but if I wanted company, I'm not short of offers. See that girl with the frizzy red hair?'

'Sipping champagne with the toff in the top hat?'

'Sweet child wouldn't leave me alone, until she found out I was broke. In fact, since I've been here, I've been propositioned by women old enough to be my mother, men wearing more face paint than a Limehouse whore, a young lady wearing nothing but a sprig of rosemary across her — well, never mind where. The point is, this glass makes for perfect companionship, and I know you feel sorry for me, but today's my day off, and without wishing to be rude, I don't need your sympathy.'

Only a policeman can stretch one day into a week. 'Without wishing to be rude either, the chemicals in my darkroom hold more appeal than the stuff you're knocking back.'

'Taste better, probably. But as you've no doubt gathered, the owner of this fine establishment is French, and while I suspect he's on first name terms with every pimp, safe-cracker and forger in Soho, it still means his wines are French, his liqueurs are French, his dancers are French —'

'With thighs like donkeys'.'

'— and —' His grey eyes shot her a now-now-don't-be-catty look — 'since I can't stomach Chartreuse, and champagne is beyond this humble detective's means, I'm reduced to —'

'Liquefied aniseed balls.'

'Pernod. And, please. Pretty as your bloodhound nose is, I beg you not to wrinkle it. If the green fairy was good enough for Byron, Baudelaire and Vincent Van Gogh, it's good enough for me.'

Bitter. Addictive. Hallucinogenic, Julia believed. Oblivion in a glass.

He tipped her a toast. 'Cures malaria, too.'

'Rife around Soho, is it?'

'Or prevents it. I forget.'

She imagined he forgot a lot of things lately. Unfortunately, not nearly enough.

Once again, she moved her chair to block his view, fluffing her leg o'mutton sleeves this time to make sure.

Once again, he moved his, but though his eyes followed the swirl of tassels and frills, they held no interest. 'Mind telling me how a respectable lady photographer wheedled her way inside this exclusive men-only establishment?'

For which read seedy, men-only dive. 'I convinced the thug at the door how it's the Bolivian ambassador's birthday, he's here incognito with friends, and —' she tapped her Box Brownie camera, useless for portraits but an otherwise all-round useful prop — 'my job is to record the event.'

'How many noughts in a bollivion?'

Julia folded her hands on the table to stop her fingers from drumming. Words couldn't reach him, neither could black-booted ankles twisting circles in the air. Swallowing her irritation, she watched him place the filigree spoon across the top of his glass, position a sugar cube in the hollow, then drip absinthe over it. The liquid turned from green to milky white when he added water.

Three glasses down the line — by which time the fug was thicker, the contortions more bawdy, and the laughter five times as coarse — Collingwood leaned across. 'All right. Why *did* you come here?'

Finally! 'Remember the baby who was kidnapped in Broadhurst? The one where the ransom wasn't collected, and the boy never found?'

Eight years dropped away in an instant. 'Thomas Forbes.'

'That's the one. Well, guess what?'

Collingwood sat up in his chair. 'He's alive?'

'No. I mean, I don't know. That's not why I wasted half a day trying to find you.' Thrown by his sudden sobriety, it came over sharper than she intended. 'It's the boy's father.'

'Austin? What about him?'

'Someone shot him twice in the back and the leg at close range with a shotgun. Your sergeant called me this morning to take scene of crime photos.'

CHAPTER 2

Darkrooms are great keepers of secrets. Far beyond the alchemy of turning base metal to gold — or in Julia's case, silver bromide into portraits — her darkroom imprisoned all manner of intimacies.

Negatives of half-naked girls with come-to-bed eyes, hinting at what the viewer was missing. Of what happens when they need satisfaction and there's no one around to oblige. Of fresh-faced innocents testing the bath water with a delicate toe, along with a sequence of images, which, when flicked through at speed, showed girls teasing their clothes off. Secrets which, until recently, Julia kept in a rented darkroom on the far side of the town. Cancelling the lease on her darkroom was a decision she'd regretted almost at once, but, until she found new premises, and recruited enough new models to cover the expense after severing ties with her old ones, it was a decision she had to live with. Even if it was hand-to-mouth.

Other confidences were kept here. Men, whose relationships must stay hidden, or risk three years' hard labour for gross indecency. Romeo-and-Juliets, commissioning portraits behind their warring families' backs. Couples blasted by both Church and the law as adulterers, but when you're locked in a truly miserable marriage, what's wrong with finding happiness and joy outside it? Last, but not least though, Julia's darkroom held secrets that only the dead can reveal.

Photographing the murder scene with an artist's eye that captures every nuance, she'd been able to piece together the last moments of murder victims. Some were straightforward deductions. The fact that the most recent death was after an appointment, rather than an assignation, for example, as proved by the typewritten note sticking out of Austin Forbes' pocket. *Windmill Hill. Half past seven. Important developments.* The time of death was sixteen minutes to eight, thanks to the watch that smashed when the first blast sent him flying. She'd taken a close-up of the cracked face to preserve the evidence, the same way she'd photographed the typewritten note, in case the ink smudged or the note fell out when the body was stretchered away. What was going through Austin's mind when he'd been checking the time, though? Was he worried the other party had forgotten? Annoyed at being kept waiting —?

Windmill Hill was a local beauty spot, offering panoramic views of the countryside to the west, and as such, a favourite spot for picnickers, lovers and factory workers who could watch sunsets that weren't blocked out by smoke. Setting up her tripod that morning, Julia tried to picture it from the dead man's perspective. The sun would have been rising behind him, scenting the air with berries and smoky wild mushrooms from the woods. Across the valley, the bells of St. Michael would have been tolling the faithful to morning prayer. Maybe even the same buzzard that circled overhead as she'd focused was soaring above the patchwork of orchards and fields at the time.

Did Austin know straight off that he'd been shot, or did he just think he'd tripped? A sticky pool testified to how much blood gushed from the back of his thigh, which she'd recorded from three separate angles, defining the spot where he'd made a tourniquet from his neck-tie and wrapped his frock coat round the wound to protect it.

Did he hear the chuff of a locomotive in the distance? See the clouds of white steam billowing above the tree line as the

7.37am ferried passengers from Broadhurst to Oakbourne, then on to London? So near and yet so far?

Julia's photographs recorded the bloody trail where he'd dragged himself through the grass, dirty elbows testimony to the method. Again, so near and yet so far, because while he was hauling himself back to his horse, fire ripping through every sinew and bone, the second barrel discharged.

And that time Austin would have known he hadn't tripped.

After leaving Collingwood, Julia had caught the train back to Oakbourne, pushing images of the victim, face down in a mess of his own shattered organs, to the edge of her mind. As the train chugged westwards, she concentrated instead on what she'd gleaned about Austin Forbes from the officers at the scene, and for a man who didn't come from their patch, they seemed to know pretty much everything there was to know! Partly, she imagined, because his jams had earned a Royal Warrant. An accolade neither Hartley's nor Mr. Wilkin's 'Tiptree' preserves had achieved. But mainly, she supposed, because millionaire factory owners couldn't keep low profiles even if they wanted.

Especially when their sons vanish without trace.

'Penny? Penny, sir? Help a half-blind, homeless soldier?'

Sweeping out from the station, dodging horses, bicycles, dray carts and carriages, Julia collided with a beggar accosting passengers flocking off the train.

'Penny? Penny, miss? Help a half-blind, homeless soldier?'

She took stock of his fine sandy hair, the wiry frame in frayed, ill-fitting clothes, the patch over his right eye, the croaky voice, and the shaky hand holding the cap. 'Absolutely.' What was he? Thirty-five? Forty? 'I'd consider it an honour.'

Leaning in, she lifted a penny from his cap and set a brisk pace up the hill.

'*Oi! Give that back, you* —' Whatever names he called her were drowned by the whistle of the guard, the whoosh of steam, and the clank of wheels on metal, but he made no attempt to follow. Too many other passengers to pester, and in the crowd of silks and feathers, big hats and big sleeves, parasols and canes, she'd have been swallowed up long before he turned the corner.

Tossing the coin in the air and catching it as she crossed Oakbourne Common, Julia reflected that, considering she didn't have access to a specialised tripod like the Parisian police employed, her system for capturing crime scenes was proving pretty damn effective. Under the oak trees, squirrels burrowed in the leaf litter for acorns to take away and bury, ducks quacked on the pond. Of course, the reason she hadn't been provided with equipment specifically designed to photograph corpses from above was because the practice wasn't even acknowledged, much less recognised, in British law. The Metropolitan Police had experimented a few times, most notably during the Jack the Ripper investigations seven years ago, but whether, like fingerprinting, it was dismissed because the most notorious killer in living memory slipped through the net, she'd never know. The point is, the Home Office continued to insist that the primary role of the police was crime prevention, ruling crime scene photography a futile waste of time and resources, and best left to the French.

It was only DI John Collingwood — relentless, ambitious, a wolf in wolf's clothing — who saw the benefits of preserving murder scenes before evidence could be contaminated, trampled, discarded or destroyed. After all, constables patrolling at the regulation two-and-a-half miles an hour might be able to crack down on burglary, vagrancy and prostitution, making the streets a safer place to walk, but you're never going to stamp out rape and murder. In these instances, and with Collingwood's sights set firmly on promotion, photographic records became the perfect complement to often imprecise notes jotted down by his officers in the rush of the moment, and witnesses memories that invariably became less and less reliable over time. Because if one thing was guaranteed to propel a DI up the ladder, it was making every case that he presented in court lock, stock and barrel watertight.

So while Julia's role was anything but official, she had to say, it was bloody satisfying.

CHAPTER 3

'Christ, man.' Chief Superintendent Cuthbert Blaine gestured with the butt of his cigar for Collingwood to take a seat. 'Couldn't you at least have shaved before you came to see me?'

Collingwood clambered over a stack of archives, removed two box files from the chair and flicked away a score of loose treasury tags, before realising he'd sat in a layer of ash. 'Working undercover, sir.'

Blaine's brows met in a frown above his rimless pince-nez, but he confined himself to a grunt. 'On what?'

Collingwood tried to cross his legs. The archives fought back. He rested his feet on them instead. 'A cat burglar.'

Blaine continued to scan the report on his desk, signed it off, blotted it, then reached for the next one. 'I presume we're talking lion, rather than some scrawny feral kitten?'

'I believe so, because if I'm right, and I'm pretty sure I am, half the thefts haven't been noticed, much less reported to the police.'

Blaine scratched through a line of type and re-wrote it. 'Strikes me as hotchpotch of supposition, hunches and thin air, yet here's you, trailing all the way to Headquarters to blow this kettle of tosh in my face, rather than investigating the murder of one of the most prominent individuals this side of the Andes.'

'Every man in my command is working flat out on the Forbes shooting, but as you know, Boot Street's a small station in comparison.' Just him, two sergeants and sixteen constables working shifts.

'Are you requesting additional resources? Because if so, there's such a thing as the telephone.'

'No, sir. That's not what I'm requesting.' Another grunt, but the way Blaine chewed his cigar told Collingwood he was intrigued, even though his eyes never left the page. 'The cat burglar is only targeting the homes of the exceptionally wealthy, and in return he's exceptionally selective.'

Collingwood stared out the window across the broad, tree-lined thoroughfare two floors below shimmering with ostrich feather hats, leg o'mutton sleeves and jewel coloured silks. Impressive moustaches paraded beneath dark derby hats. Parasols twirled, phaetons clopped, and (shock, horror) could that really be ladies riding bicycles in bloomer suits?

'He confines his haul to jewels and other items that the owners rarely use or wear or show,' he continued. 'Snuff boxes, antiquities, small things like that. Inevitably, some thefts are noticed and reported — here's the list — which is how I worked out the pattern. But! Given the gentry's habit of only bringing certain pieces into play on high days and holidays, our feline friend has all the time in the world to plunder as many properties as he likes before anyone twigs. And because he doesn't steal much at a time, suspicion lands on the servants.'

Blaine's mouth twisted. 'Charming fellow.'

'Professional thieves aren't celebrated for their conscience, only their skill, and this one seems to have invested a great deal of research into his subject matter.' Collingwood paused. 'Suggesting the victims know and trust him.'

'Inside job. I like it.' Blaine signed off the report and tossed it in the tray on top of the others. 'Now explain to me how you plan to find Forbes' killer and at the same time expose a thief who is calmly cherry-picking his way through the whole of Oakbourne —'

'And beyond, actually.' Collingwood got up and opened the window, bringing the ring of bicycle bells and the smell of a flower girl's roses into the office. Far cry from Boot Street, where you either got smoke from the factories or the stink of blood and guts from the butcher's, depending which way the wind happened to be blowing. 'I've been in contact with the DCI in the adjacent jurisdiction where the cat's been equally active. Larger than Boot Street by a considerable margin, I need your permission to pool our resources, because with a joint force at our disposal —'

'Which jurisdiction?'

Collingwood didn't much care for the edge to Blaine's voice. 'Does it matter?'

'*Which fucking jurisdiction?*'

'Broadhurst.'

'No, no, no, no, no.' Blaine slammed down his fountain pen. Ink splattered everywhere. 'I knew you were bloody up to something the second you walked in, and the answer, before you even try to justify this, is no. No. Way.'

'Eight years ago, Austin's son, his only child, was abducted, the ransom never touched, and the boy never seen again. Surely that justifies inter-force co-operation?'

'Where were you, eight years ago, when that kid was taken?'

'Co-opted into the Met to work the Mile End Monster rapes.'

'Right. And I was DCI in Broadhurst when Thomas Forbes went missing, so don't you *dare* try to twist this investigation into something it's not.' Blaine's stubby finger jabbed the air. 'We pulled out every stop and then some to find that boy, none of us slept for weeks, and unless you were right there, in the thick of it, you can't begin to imagine the effect it had.'

Collingwood watched a pigeon strut along the windowsill as the light slowly faded from the sky. 'People didn't suddenly become afraid for their own children, then? Couldn't sleep for wondering if Forbes was the intended target, or their kid might be next? That a cloud of suspicion didn't spread over the entire town? Mistrust of their neighbours? Shopkeepers? Servants? Friends? Especially the workers from the East End, who flocked in to harvest the orchards?'

'Good. You can imagine.' The leather of Blaine's swivel chair creaked as he leaned forward. 'Because maybe now you can see why raking up the living hell the kidnapper put not just the Forbes, but that whole community through, won't serve any useful purpose.'

'You mean no one wants to be reminded of the massive failure on the part of the police?'

Blaine ignored that. 'They don't want to re-live their old nightmares, you arrogant moron. Now the long and short of the matter is this. Austin Forbes was never a man to win any popularity contests, and Cara Forbes has been to hell and back. Several times. Which means, as far as today's events are concerned, it's simple. Forbes failed to turn up for his appointment at the bank. His valet despatched men to look for him —'

'— they found him at on the edge of a local beauty spot, with a trail of blood leading through the grass. I'm well aware of that. But it doesn't mean the crimes aren't connected, and with two forces working together —'

'Perhaps I didn't make myself clear.' Blaine lowered his voice to a growl. 'Accidents happen. Especially in an economic climate where the rich are getting richer and the poor are — well, not to put too fine a point on it, dying like flies. God bless the Industrial Revolution, eh. The point is, you and I call hunting at a local beauty spot poaching. A man with a starving family calls it necessity. Now for God's sake, Collingwood, you concentrate on that bloody burglar, that's all, and leave the past where it belongs.'

'I agree, a man would worry how his family would survive now that … I don't know, an injury in, say, the refinery rendered him unfit to work. And, for argument's sake, let's say debility put him off his aim, in which case, he might well panic and run away. But you tell me what kind of poacher watches his quarry haul himself along on his stomach, waits while he knots his blue and white spotted neck-tie in a tourniquet, then walks up empties the barrel while he's face down, helpless as a baby, and watches him writhe in agony for however long it takes for his lungs to fill with blood and shards of his own backbone.'

'Jesus Christ!' Blaine's eyes bounced off his spectacles. 'Your sergeant's memorandum had it listed as an accident.'

'On my instructions. Like you say, panic serves no useful purpose, either.'

'This is what is going to happen.' Blaine slammed the window shut. 'You will return to Boot Street, you will tell your men they can go home to their wives, then you will take a razor to your face and spend as much time as it takes trailing around after your little pussycat, because you're off the case.'

'You can't do that.'

'I just did.' Blaine's smile wasn't pretty. 'Before, you see, it was simply a shooting.'

'And now it's murder, I understand that. But Windmill Hill is my manor. This is my case.'

'Not any more. Forbes might have taken his last breath within Oakbourne's boundary, but only by a hundred yards. He lived in Broadhurst, owned half the bloody land there, his factories are there, he's endowed more charitable foundations than you can shake a stick at, including the Hospital for

Incurables, and if that isn't enough, there was talk of a possible knighthood. Which means I am personally overseeing this investigation, and I'll be the one liaising with DCI Dudley in Broadhurst and keeping the damned press at bay. Me. Not you. Understand? Because the last thing I need, the very, very last thing I need, is some self-pitying drunk ballsing up this case.'

'I'm not —'

'Don't take me for a fool, man. You're not bloody undercover, never were. I smelled the booze the second you walked in, and given the vagrants, drunks and whores that pass through this establishment, that's quite an achievement.' The heat of Blaine's anger congealed to contempt. 'Get out. Now. And trust me, if I ever find your men covering for you again, it won't just be you out on your arse, they'll be out of work as well. Am I clear?'

'Crystal.' Collingwood rose, and as he replaced the box files on the chair, said, 'Just remember Dudley's good...'

The cigar turned in Blaine's mouth. 'But?'

'I'm better.'

'Only when you're sober.'

Collingwood ran his fingers through his hair. To his shame, his hands were shaking. 'Wednesday was the anniversary of Alice's death,' he said. 'Getting drunk was my way of blotting it out.'

The admission caught Blaine off guard, taking all the bluster with it. 'How long since she died?'

'Four weeks.'

'Four weeks.' Blaine drew a deep breath, as though surprised at the swiftness of time, then pushed out his lower lip. 'Sweet girl, your Alice. Always ready with a smile, and pretty with it, too.' He shook his head. 'Tragedy. Absolute tragedy, losing a child so young, and her the only one. Then that ghastly business with your wife…'

'Thank you, sir, I appreciate that.'

'Don't, because it doesn't change a bloody thing. I'm sorry about what happened to your daughter, John, I truly am, and I'm sorry it drove your wife to the point where she had to be locked away. But however grievous the circumstances, we are Her Majesty's police and we have a duty to uphold. I cannot — will not — tolerate self-pitying drunks on my force. Or self-pitying teetotallers, come to that. This country, in fact the whole bloody Empire, is founded on truth and integrity, and we, as the police, are the front-line defenders of that faith. I will not see it compromised, particularly over an issue as sensitive as Austin Forbes. Now bugger off, there's a good chap.' Blaine smiled. 'Go do what you're paid to do, what we're all paid to do. Prevent crime. And while you have no idea how much I look forward to you grabbing that lion by its tail, so help me God —' the edge was back — 'if you so much as set one toe in Broadhurst's jurisdiction on the pretext of chasing jewel thieves, you'll be walking the worst beat in the force for the rest of your life.'

Since there was nothing to say, Collingwood said nothing. Drunk or sober, he knew a last chance when it saw it.

He also knew that, if he could find the truth, it would seal his promotion to DCI.

CHAPTER 4

There are many calls on a photographer's time, but arguably the most important is making sure the studio stays open, and that means paying the bills. Pulling the last of her invoices out of the typewriter, Julia folded them neatly, addressed the envelopes, then stuck on the stamps. No mean feat, when your fingers are crossed in the hope that they'll be settled swiftly. Even the church mice left handouts.

Throwing a silk shawl round her shoulders, she pinned on a small (for her) frothy little number, all wired net and swirls in canary yellow trimmed with black. Keeping up appearances was half the battle when it came to attracting clients, and hats that screamed elegance and sophistication, with just the right touch of chic, were the cavalry.

'Ha'penny, miss? Just the price of one of them stamps there, to help a half-blind, homeless soldier—*YOU?*'

Julia pushed the letters through the slot and smiled. 'Me.'

'What d'you do a rotten thing like that for yesterday? Thieving off the poor!'

'Which regiment?'

'Eh?'

'Simple question. Which regiment did this poor half-blinded, homeless soldier serve?'

'Royal Horse Guards, if yer must know. S'how I lost me voice. As a corporal barking orders.'

'Then I *must* introduce you to Sergeant Kincaid at Boot Street police station. He was with the Blues, too. Colour sergeant. Probably served at the same time.' She glanced at the watch pinned to her blouse. 'If we hurry, we should catch him. I'm sure you'll both have much to talk about.'

'All right, mebbe I exaggerated a bit. Nothing quite so prestigious as the Horse Guards.'

'Nothing quite so prestigious as the army, either.'

'You calling me a liar?' Matching her pace as she turned back, his tone was remarkably casual.

'Let's just say you don't have anything close to a military gait, plus last Friday, when you were hanging round the market, you wore an eyepatch over your left eye.'

'Blimey. Ain't you got a sharp eye and keen memory! Bet your old man can't get away with anything.'

Julia rubbed the wedding ring she'd bought after Sam Whitmore — friend, saviour, father-figure, mentor, the only man she'd ever trusted — died, forcing her to add a "Mrs" to her already fictitious name in order to run the business he bequeathed her. 'I'm a widow.'

'Sorry to hear that. What 'appened?'

And that's the problem when your whole life is a lie. There were so many falsehoods, where do you start? From where she'd killed a man to save him from killing her family to the new identity she'd created, via her sordid involvement in striptease photography, Julia had resorted to writing them down. Cheat sheet in every sense, but unless fraud comes naturally and your brain has no other calls on its resources, it's impossible to remember a fraction of the fibs.

'I don't like to talk about.' On the other hand, she was ace at that old half-gasp, sniff and dab-with-lace-hankie routine. 'Too painful.'

'Understood. Sorry I raised the subj— Is this where you work?'

'Yes.' And what d'you know? Another lie. 'I'm Sam Whitmore's assistant.'

He stepped back and looked the studio up and down. 'You wanna tell your boss to smarten the place up a bit, luv. The nobs round 'ere won't want to be seen coming out of a place with peeling paint and flaking plaster.' He prodded one of the window frames. 'And if he don't get that rotten woodwork fixed PDQ, pardon my French, the whole bloody lot'll need replacing.'

Julia shuddered at the estimates she'd been given for painting and repair. At those prices, quite frankly she'd have expected them to rebuild the Taj Mahal, plaster the nose back on the Sphinx, and paint the Statue of Liberty for good measure. Payment for her services as Boot Street's crime scene photographer barely covered the cost of materials, and in any case, murders weren't exactly thick on the ground in this genteel jurisdiction. Which left her reliant on portraits to cover the bills, and the beggar was right. Fewer and fewer clients came calling, now that the summer sun had stripped off the last of the varnish and faded the paint. Circles rarely come more vicious.

'Fancy a cup of tea?' Anything to change the subject from money. Or rather, lack of it. No, let's be honest. Living a lie makes for unspeakable loneliness.

'Fort you'd never ask!' He grinned. 'Billy Briggs.' He held out his hand.

'Julia McAllister,' she said, returning the handshake. 'One sugar or two?'

Austin Forbes's obituary in the *Oakbourne Chronicle* reflected the image he had cultivated in life. Refined, restrained and reflective.

The usual flattering photograph to catch the eye. A glowing account of his contribution to the food processing industry, ranging from the excellence of his conserves — "*No place like home, no jam like Forbes*" — to the initiatives he had led during this terrible agricultural depression, via his passion for all aspects of fruit farming, harvest and production. The obituary made no mention of abducted children, merely listing his age as fifty-five and ending with the briefest of notes about the widow, Cara, née Hinchcliffe, that he'd left behind, before gushing how the deceased would be sorely missed by everyone in Broadhurst and beyond.

While the kettle boiled, Julia studied the fine, chiselled cheekbones in the photograph. The clipped grey beard. The backbone that could double as a ramrod. There was, she noticed, not an ounce of fat on Austin's stylishly tailored frame. Or as much as the hint of a smile. The article portrayed him as a distinguished businessman, devoted husband, and perfectionist in his trade. In short, a fine upstanding citizen, of whom the neighbouring town of Broadhurst was proud, and maybe — just maybe — that was true.

But when a man is shot twice, both times with his back turned, it raises all manner of questions. Questions that Julia believed she could help answer.

She warmed the teapot. Doled out the aromatic leaves from the caddy. Last night, fresh from his call on the chief superintendent, Collingwood relayed how he'd been warned off the case. She didn't blame him for turning to drink. His only child had died in horrific circumstances, lumbering him with a wife in an asylum, who he could never divorce, while costing him his house, his hopes and his dreams in the process. Unfortunately, through the bottle, he was risking the only thing he had left. His job. Julia was damned if she'd let him lose that as well.

Blaine never warned civilian photographers off the case.

'You said tea. You never said nothing about slap-up breakfasts.'

'I haven't eaten this morning, Billy Briggs, and I'm pretty sure you haven't either, so please don't make me waste these eggs.'

'No chance!' He tucked in with gusto — and surprisingly good manners. 'This uncle's delicious.'

Was that why he was begging? The asylum he'd escaped from was holding his money? 'I cook cousins on Mondays, aunts on a Tuesday, but I only roast uncles on Sundays.'

'Rhyming slang, luv. Uncle Fred: bread.' He grinned. 'Unless you mean the missionary captured by cannibals in the jungle, where they got their first taste of religion.'

'You'll probably go to hell for that.'

'Already got me ticket.'

Julia strained more tea into her cup. 'Come on, then. If you weren't in the army, what were you before you took to the road?'

'How d'you know homeless isn't another whopper?'

Grey skin. Broken fingernails. Dirt ingrained so deep on hands it didn't wash out in the sink, even with a scrubbing brush. A voice croaky from too many cigarettes and not enough sleep. All those might just indicate a man not taking care of himself. But oh, the haunting sadness in those pale blue eyes...

'Just a hunch.' She reached for another slice of ham, wishing she could break this habit of picking up waifs and strays. Except she'd been there herself. Experienced the desolation first hand, the loneliness, and the fear. Was it for them — or herself — that she helped them? 'And stop changing the subject.'

Billy shot her a sharp sideways glance. 'No flies on you, is there.' He munched his way through another half a slice then emptied his cup, but Julia knew he was reflecting, not stalling. 'Don't laugh, I trained as a glove-maker.'

'Need a hand?'

'You palming me off with unskilled labour?'

'I'd get a-wristed.'

'Only if I fingered you for the job.'

'I'd still glove you, though.' She rolled her eyes. 'You've heard them all, haven't you?'

'Yeah, but —' he sighed. 'Not for a long, long, long, long time.' He waggled his threadbare trousers and ragged, patched-up jacket. 'These days, I'm a grass inspector.'

'Grass. Inspector.'

'Y'know what they say — always greener on the other side. Someone has to test the theory, dontcha think?'

She watched him mop up the last of his breakfast with his bread. 'And is it?'

'Beats waitin' round to die.' He shot her what she realised was his trademark sideways look. 'Figuratively speaking, o'course. Don't want you to think I've left something contagious behind as payment for me grub.'

'Grub's on the house.'

'Really?' Blue eyes twinkled. 'In that case, any chance of another cuppa?'

CHAPTER 5

BABY KIDNAPPED!

Three nights ago, 17-month-old Thomas Forbes, son of jam tycoon Austin Forbes, was snatched from his cot in Chislehurst Hall.

According to police reports, Thomas was put to bed at his normal hour by his nurse. She left him for just a few minutes, to run one of her regular errands. When she returned, the baby was gone.

News of the crime only broke when Mr. Forbes reported his son's disappearance yesterday evening. Detective Chief Inspector Blaine rushed to the scene, where he was shown the ransom note left on Thomas's pillow.

Mr. Forbes explained how he had followed the kidnappers' demands to leave the money, rumoured to be in the region of a thousand pounds, at the folly in the grounds of his estate. The note insisted that, if he wanted to see his son again, Mr. Forbes must obey the instructions and not contact the police. This he did, to the letter. When he failed to receive any communication from the kidnappers after three days, he returned to the folly. The money hadn't been touched.

Speaking for the police, DCI Blaine confirmed there was no sign of forced entry at Chislehurst Hall, but added that the harvesting of the orchards, as well as all the different berries, is a notoriously busy period, with hundreds of itinerant workers flooding the region. With this spell of warm weather, any one of them could have slipped in through an open window without being seen. The house and grounds have been searched for clues, but the police admit they have found nothing that might lead to an arrest. Dogs have been brought in to search the woods and surrounding area. The ornamental lake is being drained.

The date of the newspaper was September 15th 1887, but it quickly became clear that the archives in Julia's local library were seriously deficient when it came to in-depth reporting. If she was to understand what happened two years prior to her and Sam Whitmore pitching tent here, she needed to go to the place where it all started — and since the bus to Broadhurst had just left, and the next train wasn't for another two hours, there was only one option. Dust off the bicycle, don the bottle green velvet bloomer suit, and pedal over before the iron became too cold to strike.

Why can't a bicycle stand up on its own? It's two tyred.
Why don't bank managers ride a bicycle? They lose their balance.
How did the barber win the cycle race? He took a short cut.

Swapping music hall jokes was more than a means of her and Sam passing time in the days when plates needed to be developed within ten minutes of taking pictures and photography was an itinerant trade. It was Sam's way of giving Julia back her childhood, showing her that being happy wasn't something to feel guilty or ashamed of, and that people weren't defined by what they had done. Only by what they did next.

Oh, Sam! Do you have any idea how wise you are?
Did the little piggy go wee-wee-wee all the way home?

Must be the smoke from the starch mills making her eyes water, because Sam always knew how to make her laugh. But, hey presto, before she knew it, the stench from the meat paste factories and soap works was behind her and sunlight that had been blocked by a crowd of distilleries, gas works and refineries streamed down on the rich, fertile soil fed by the Thames. Instead of sulphur and soot, the air was impregnated with the scent of ripe pears and apples, plums and blackberries, alive with song from the workers harvesting the fruit.

If there was one thing experience as a police photographer had taught Julia McAllister, it was how all five senses came into play at a crime scene. Professionally, she'd concentrate on slotting plates in the camera, lining up the shots and capturing the scene from as many angles as possible before evidence was contaminated, lost or destroyed. No matter how hard you try, though, you can't block out the stench of blood, or the taste of decomposition in the back of your throat. No amount of whisky can wash that away, she had tried, while the sight of bloated flesh and staring eyes haunted her dreams. Yet it's those very sensory perceptions that help piece the puzzle together, and while this was hardly her first visit to Broadhurst, those freshly heightened senses emphasised exactly how modern the town was.

Oakbourne had evolved from ancient aristocratic seats along with ecclesiastical establishments that had grown slowly as the centuries unfolded. Broadhurst took a shortcut. With no canal to introduce industry at a leisurely pace, it simply sprang up when the railways arrived, and continued to prosper and boom. Consequently, it was home to an entirely new kind of elite. One in which get-rich-quick trumped nobility, and breeding proved no match for business acumen.

With this fresh perspective, Julia studied the theatre's arched windows, stone carvings and balconies. A box at the Royal Opera House in London would set the average worker back a hundred years' salary. Here, among the elegant, tree-lined streets flanked by stately mansions, she imagined it would only be fifty.

Those same heightened perceptions scanned perambulators being pushed round the park, while little girls skipped by with a rope, boys played tag round the oak trees, and dogs chased pigeons they'd never catch. Was it a trick of the light, or did the shopkeepers in Broadhurst have cleaner aprons than Oakbourne? Smarter armbands round their sleeves? Stiffer collars? And what looked like brand new straw hats all round?

By and large, people take one look at the smog that blankets most industrialised towns, and equate machinery with progress and profit. How many stopped to consider how the high wages that lured workers away from the farms barely covered their rent, food and heat? That city prices were far in excess of country prices, forcing the poor sods to sleep eight or ten to one dingy cramped room, rife with crime and disease? Were the men, whose steam-driven machines bought their incredible mansions, aware of their workers' living conditions? Of course they were.

Did they care? Did they hell.

Julia leaned her bicycle against the railings of the *Broadhurst Gazette*, and trusted to the usual combination of stylish modern looks, her faithful Box Brownie camera — and, all right, maybe, just maybe, that shiny silver sixpence — to bluff her way down the spiral metal staircase into the archives. Here, by the light of a spitting gas lamp, and surrounded by mouse droppings, yellowed newsprint and dust thick enough to stand a teacup on, she brushed millennia of cobwebs from the only serviceable chair, opened her notebook and boned up on the events that took place eight years ago.

FEARS GROW!

With no clues yet as to the whereabouts of the missing baby, Thomas Forbes, detectives nevertheless remain optimistic that the child is alive.

Believing something went wrong with the ransom collection that prevented the kidnappers from reaching the folly, efforts have been concentrated on the labourers who descend every year to help harvest the crops.

'I am convinced Thomas is being held somewhere in the vicinity,' DCI Blaine insisted. 'Wherever he is, you can rest assured we will find him.'

As news of the kidnapping spread, help has been flooding in from the public. One witness reported seeing a boy tied up in a barn. Police immediately rushed to the scene, where, unfortunately, it turned out to be a hoax.

'I don't know who would play such a terrible trick,' Mr. Forbes told the Gazette. 'But I thank all those kind and genuine people who have thrown themselves into the search.'

He went on to offer a hundred pound reward for the recovery of his son. Dead or alive.

It is common knowledge that his neighbour, Mr. Henry Davenport of Lindale Manor, recently gifted Mr. Forbes a large portion of his estate, including fields and farmlands, along with the famous Davenport orchards. Equally well-documented was Mr. Davenport's suicide almost immediately after the transfer became official. When questioned about these events by the Gazette, and asked whether, in his opinion, the kidnap might have a more personal motive, Mr. Forbes replied, 'The acquisition of that land is my business. How the Davenports react to change of ownership is theirs.'

Mrs. Forbes has remained indoors throughout the ordeal. Looking drawn and pale, the only comment she has made to the press has been, 'God will take care of my son, I just know it.'

We all pray she is right.

Lamplight bounced off the spiral staircase, reminding Julia of the shadow puppets her mother made on the wall when she was little. Closing her eyes, she could smell the violets of her perfume, and when she opened them again, she half-expected to hear her rich peals of laughter as she made foxes, geese and rabbits dance across the ceiling.

Until one cold, damp February night, when different shadows started dancing.

That was the first time Julia had witnessed her stepfather beat her mother, but in that moment, she knew it wasn't the first time it had happened.

'I slipped on the path, lovey, that's all.'

'Clumsy old me, tripped over the coal bucket.'

'Who put that door there, eh?'

Bruises, limps and bumps that had been dismissed with a roll of eyes and silly-me giggle took on a different slant that night.

Julia was barely seven years old.

Damn. She unpinned her boater, tweaked the brim, fiddled with the ribbon, then laid it on the second stair, as though neatness would somehow drive away the demon. But since demons have no manners, she flipped back to that fourth-from-last paragraph.

It is common knowledge that his neighbour, Mr. Henry Davenport of Lindale Manor, recently gifted Mr. Forbes a large portion of his estate, including fields and farmlands, along with the famous Davenport orchards. Equally well-documented was Mr. Davenport's suicide almost immediately after the transfer became official.

That had to be a misprint?

Apparently not. And it didn't take long to learn all there was to know about this mysterious benefactor, because what do you know? Henry Davenport's profile turned out to be even higher than Austin's. Here, at last, was good old-fashioned landed gentry, who, according to the records, lived in Lindale Manor with his second wife, Lydia, widowed daughter Alexandra, and granddaughter, Grace. He was not a member of the peerage, but nevertheless came from a family that had owned and farmed the land since —

'Oh, for God's sake!' Julia exclaimed aloud.

That was just about the biggest load of balls she'd read in her entire life. No one, and she meant absolutely no one, gifts three centuries of hard graft to a neighbour! The effort of trying to make sense of it was making her head ache, but she couldn't give up now, she owed it to Collingwood, and the best way to get a handle on this sordid drama was to list everything down, thereby putting it into some kind of context from which to work. Opening her notebook, she began to write.

1. Cheap American wheat floods the market, driving down prices and forcing arable farming to the brink of extinction.

All right, all right, maybe not extinction, but the impact was pretty bloody dire. The constant drop in wheat prices, currently at their lowest level in 150 years, had thrown British agriculture into a depression it was unlikely to crawl out from. Rather than file for bankruptcy, fall into poverty, end up in the workhouse or sell off their lands, many farmers turned to different practices. In Suffolk, for example, they'd switched from wheat to cattle and sheep.

2. At the same time, British goods are in such demand worldwide, and mechanisation is moving so fast, that virtually every factory, dock and mill up and down the country is desperate for workers.

3. With pay far in excess of anything they can earn at home, agricultural labourers flood the cities.

Despite the atrocious living conditions!

4. Rapidly expanding cities need to be fed.

5. Broadhurst, in tandem with Isleworth in Middlesex, becomes the fruit and vegetable garden of London.

6. Land prices, then, must be at a premium?

Well beyond aching, Julia's head was thumping like a kettledrum. Blame the heavy iron presses clunking overhead? The chatter of Smith Premier typewriters in the outer office, belting out a thousand keys a minute? The telegraph machine, that clacked like a pair of badly fitting dentures? Nice try. Land prices at a premium, yet shortly before his son was abducted, Austin acquired huge tracts of his neighbour's property without payment changing hands, plunging the previously wealthy Davenports into poverty. Then turned the fruits of his new labours quite literally into profit in the form of jam production, growing richer and ever more successful.

'Not in a million years,' she muttered. 'Not in a million bloody years do I believe a word of this.'

And another thing! She double-checked to make sure, but yes, that's what the article said. *Davenport recently gifted...* Recently my eye. We're talking newspapers — journalists — sensationalism — the need to sell copies. If the transaction was that fresh, they'd have said so!

She stretched out her arms. Arched her back. Yawned. If the stench of oil, ink and hot metal seeping down from the print room bothered her, it didn't show. No one had followed the galloping advances in photography closer than Julia McAllister, advances that went light years beyond replacing plates in a camera with strips of film. Flip books and peep shows (technically folioscopes and kinetoscopes, but who calls them that?) were all the rage now. Especially when they revealed young women teasing their clothes off. Magic lantern shows —

technically zoetropes, but who in their right mind ties their tongue round that? And even more exciting, between the Lumière Brothers on this side of the Atlantic and Thomas Edison on the other, motion pictures were already having their first public screenings.

Alongside, though, another revolutionary process was underway which, if her maths were correct, would allow fifteen million words to fit on a single square inch, meaning a one-foot cube could contain a staggering one and a half million volumes. Sadly, microform photography had not yet made the jump to meaningful employment, and certainly not in the newspaper world. Flicking away another mouse dropping, Julia undid the top two buttons of her blouse and, with a sigh, waded deeper into the yellowing paper mountain.

Deeper, and deeper, and deeper.

Scanning columns, flipping through endless political commentaries, carriage accidents and obituaries, she almost missed it —

But. February 23rd, in the Year of our Lord 1887, seven months before Thomas was abducted, there it was. Overshadowed by an earthquake off the Mediterranean coast — the strongest ever recorded, in which two thousand poor souls perished, including three hundred who'd taken refuge in a church — the death of Henry Davenport barely rated a mention. Why should it? Six in the morning, pitch black, thousands of people lost their homes, their possessions, their livestock, their pets. Buildings tumbled like cards, including the Ducal Palace in Genoa, a tidal wave swamped the Riviera, there were landslides and aftershocks, and to cap it all Bertie, Prince of Wales, was in Cannes at the time, celebrating *Mardi Gras*.

Look hard enough, though, and you see a tiny piece tucked away on page 20, relating how, after signing away his fields and orchards to his neighbour, Henry Davenport went home, closed the door to his office, and promptly blew his brains out. The article confirmed the rumours that no money changed hands, which, in itself, you'd think was newsworthy enough to make the front page, never mind the suicide of Broadhurst's number one son. What set the prickles rising on Julia's neck was the weapon he used to despatch himself.

A double-barrelled shotgun.

Rubbing eyes made dry from all these dusty papers, she suddenly saw the dimples in her mother's cheeks when she smiled. Smelled the gravy of her rich stargazey pies, so named because the heads of the sardines pushed up through the crumbly pastry, "gazing at the stars". Remembered the way she held the notes when she sang *Sweet Nightingale* to rock Julia to sleep. Could almost reach out and stroke the kitten her mother gave her for her birthday.

With a flicker of the oil lamp, the moment passed. Now it was the tortured expressions of the men who'd wheeled her father's broken body home in a barrow that she saw. The same men who'd hauled him up from the bottom of the mine shaft when he fell. Dear God, would it ever fade, the sight of the blood draining from her mother's face as the eviction notice was served just three days later? The sick sensation in her stomach that came from knowing she and her brother were too young to work, even by modern standards, leaving the widow with no choice but to align herself to the only man who offered her his hand? A sly, sadistic predator, who'd sought her out purely because she was vulnerable, and knew she'd put up with anything rather than see her children in the workhouse.

Twelve years on, in the stillness of the night, Julia still found herself shaking uncontrollably at the pleasure in his eyes while he squeezed the life oh-so-slowly from the kitten. Not at killing it. At the pain it caused a little girl.

It wasn't long before he took his belt and fists to the widow's son, saving a different weapon entirely for the daughter. The weapon he kept in his trousers. In fact, it was only when he'd beaten his wife to the point where her jaw shattered, leaving her unable to speak, and her cheekbones smashed so she couldn't open her eyes, and the son crippled, most likely for life, that Julia saw a way out.

It wasn't a double-barrelled shotgun.

But it had bullets that found their mark.

Stop. She wiped eyes that had miraculously acquired moisture. The past is past, and this is not the time! With a deep but shaky breath, she returned to the events of eight years before. *If it bleeds, it leads* was the old newspaper adage, and a little boy's disappearance would have shifted a lot of papers at the time. But as summer faded and autumn moved to winter, leads dried up, clues petered out and press coverage became less and less. By Christmas, there wasn't so much as a mention of Thomas. It was as though the child had never existed.

She drummed her pencil against the arm of the chair. Perhaps it was the memories? Her mother... Her brother... The ghosts of happy times fading with every day that passed...

Perhaps it was the injustice. That life was neither fair nor evenly distributed, and that baby Thomas had deserved so much better.

Perhaps it was because this case was the only thing that would jerk Collingwood from the brink of self-destruction.

It didn't matter. A child was missing. A mother was in pain.

High time those scales were balanced.

CHAPTER 6

Extinguishing the oil lamp, Julia left the basement of the *Broadhurst Gazette* to the spiders and the mice and made a beeline for the alleyways behind the shops. What better way to fill in the background than from local people? There were always deliverymen at work somewhere, and unsurprisingly there was only one topic of conversation.

'Poaching accident, my arse. More likely one of the poor buggers Forbes drove out of business,' the grocer said, heaving a sack of flour onto his shoulder.

'Wouldn't you snap, if you ended up bankrupt through no fault of your own and lost everything?' The delivery man tossed down another sack, and no one noticed the young woman fiddling with her bicycle chain.

'Or a jealous husband.' The grocer wiped flour off his face with his forearm. 'Screwed creditors and women in equal measure, did Austin, and that, my friend, is no mean feat. How many sacks is that, mate? And while we're at it, can I add three more to next week's order?'

At the back of the Red Lion, kegs of beer were being discharged.

'It's them three workers I feel sorry for.'

'The ones he sacked on Christmas Eve?'

'How hard does a heart have to be, to turn families out on their ear like that?'

'I heard at least one of them faced him down.'

'And look how that turned out! Being beaten to within an inch of his life, poor sod. Spent Christmas and New Year in the hospital, then another week after that.'

Clearly Austin Forbes and Genghis Khan would have got along like a house on fire, but while back alleys are fine when it comes to male perspective, what Julia needed was balance. There are always two sides to a story, and where better to find the other side than a haberdashery? Three minutes, five customers, and a yard of overpriced pink ribbon later, hatpins and crochet hooks were forgotten as the two assistants gossiped while Julia pretended to browse.

'Stubborn so-and-so, Old Man Forbes.'

'Never overturned a decision in his life.'

'The staff in Chislehurst Hall walk on eggshells.'

'I'll say one thing for him.' The younger of the two assistants leaned forward. 'Never laid a hand on his wife.'

'Honestly, Edna, you can be such a clot at times.' Behind the polished counter, piled high with reels of ribbon, spools of thread, laces for corsets, laces for boots, the second assistant reached into the drawer to lay out a choice of cotton gloves. 'Classy ladies like her don't go round advertising their bruises.'

I slipped on the path, lovey, that's all.

Clumsy old me, tripped over the coal bucket.

Who put that door there, eh?

'Wonder what'll happen to the business,' Edna was saying. 'No sons. No heirs. No nothing.' No place like home, no jam like Forbes.

'Can't see Mrs. F taking over.'

'You never know what a person's capable of, till their back's against the wall.'

'Can't speak for the wall.' Edna sniggered. 'But her back's not been against his mattress for twenty years.'

'Oh, and how exactly would you know that? Tell you herself, did she?'

'Sneer all you like, but that's what my sister says, and she works for the milliner, the one who's doing a fitting for Mrs. F at two o'clock.'

'You pulling my leg?'

'Not at all. Mrs. F is never — and my sister means never — late.'

'About her and Austin not sharing a bed, you dope!'

'Oh, *that*. Well, the thing is, confidences get exchanged at establishments like that, and, promise not to pass it on, but I know for a fact he walked away from the marriage bed the night of Mrs. F's twenty-fifth birthday.'

'Some birthday present, eh?'

'I know what I'd do, if my old man pulled a stunt like that. Two bricks,' the second assistant clapped her hands together loudly, 'and any thoughts he had of playing around would be over in a jiffy.'

'With a face like his, dear, I'd have said they were over years ago,' Edna quipped, sending the two assistants into fits of giggles that led to banter which, while amusing, changed the subject completely.

On the other hand, a visit to the ironmonger's, then the chemist's, followed by lunch of a rather tasty Welsh rarebit in the Bedford Hotel allowed Julia to pick up loads of other snippets, all painting the same unpleasant picture.

Austin Forbes was a bastard, who treated his workers like dirt and his wife even worse. Not so much a question of who'd want him dead. More who wouldn't. But even bastards have a weak point, Julia thought, and Thomas was his. There had to have been at least one moment of reconciliation between him and his wife. His son was the proof.

So, rounding off with a slice of the hotel's famous blackcurrant pie, she'd calmly plotted the best way to ambush

Cara outside the milliner's at two o'clock because *Mrs. F is never — and my sister means never — late.* Yes, you could argue that spinning the poor woman a pack of lies when she was at her lowest was on a par with kicking puppies. But if a bit of trickery brought Cara peace of mind and found justice for her son, surely she would forgive any amount of subterfuge and lies.

Julia's regret was never about killing her stepfather. It was letting his brutality continue unchecked. Far from saving her mother and brother by killing him, it was because she hadn't intervened earlier that made her, and her alone, responsible for their suffering, so yes. She knew *exactly* what Cara Forbes had gone — and still was — going through.

'Oh my goodness, I'm so sorry!'

Julia rushed to catch the elegant creature she'd knocked flying outside the milliner's, and that was another difference between Broadhurst and Oakbourne. Virtually half the middle-aged women in this town sported widows' weeds, another consequence of Broadhurst's ridiculous wealth. With too much time on their hands, it seemed rich men had nothing better to do than eat themselves to death.

'Are you all right?'

Was it anger, irritation, pain or plain misery that sparked a narrowing of the eyes behind the veil? The pursing of the lips, the tensing of the spine as she straightened the hat Julia had knocked askew? 'I'm fine,' the woman said, pulling the silk tulle back in place and fluffing the black lace at her throat. 'Honestly.'

'I should have looked where I was going.'

'We both should, but —' the woman stepped back to take in Julia's outfit — 'if that was the case, I'd never have met the Gibson Girl in person.'

Julia laughed. 'Hardly.' With upswept hair and reflective expression, the Gibson Girl was the artist's definition of today's ideal young woman, setting trends in fashion, sports and social skills.

'Nonsense. You're straight off the June cover of *Scribner's Magazine*.'

'Give or take an American accent.'

'Practice makes perfect — oh, an amateur photographer, as well.'

'Professional, actually.' Julia stopped dusting off her Box Brownie where it had rolled into the gutter, and fished out a business card from her pocket.

'Whitmore Photographic? You're a long way from Oakbourne, Miss … Whitmore, I assume?'

'McAllister, and it's Mrs. I'm Mr. Whitmore's assistant, and the reason I cycled over on my afternoon off is because I'd heard this establishment is the best for hats.'

'In my opinion, they are better than the best.' The stranger held out a hand encased in black lace. 'Cara Forbes —'

'Mrs. Forbes!' Julia clamped an apologetic hand over her mouth. 'Once again, I'm so dreadfully sorry. I didn't realise, or I wouldn't have been so crass as to make light at such a terrible time. My condolences. How are you holding up, you poor thing?'

Exhausted, angry, terrified, helpless. How else did the widows of murder victims hold up, with the added agony of their lost son propelled into focus?

'I've been better.' A shuddering sigh came from behind the veil. 'To be honest, I don't think it's sunk in yet.'

Best way, because the longer Cara kept reality at bay, the easier it was to pretend nothing had happened. Anything, *anything*, than stir up the pain of the past.

'I understand,' Julia said. Was she overplaying this? 'I'm a widow myself —'

'You won't know what it's like to face it alone, though! Not to have a family round you, no friends, no —'

'As a matter of fact, I know exactly what that's like.'

'You *do*?' Some of the pain drained out of the older woman's voice. 'It would be less of a trial, if the vultures of the press would leave me alone. They love nothing more, it seems, than to pick at the carcass of grief and distress.'

The tensing up, the pursed lips, the ripple of alarm became clear. 'You thought I was a reporter. Sending you flying as an excuse for gaining an interview.'

Cara flicked a nervous glance up and down the street. 'They're making my life a misery. I had no choice but to come into town today, but even there, I was forced to sneak out like a thief from my own house.'

Dressmakers, armed with fabric samples and tape measures for funeral attire, will happily pay house calls. Unfortunately, with hats the size they were today, Mohammed had no choice other than to come to the mountain, and that's the drawback with wealth. Even in the shadow of the Grim Reaper, one still has one's position to uphold.

'Eight years ago, my husband shielded me from those jackals.'

Cara lifted her veil to look Julia in the eye, and any images Julia had drawn in her mind — dowdy, plain, undoubtedly plump — popped like a bubble. With her strong cheekbones, swan neck and firm jawline, in the right light this woman could pass for fifteen years younger. Murder, unfortunately, didn't cast the right light.

Even so, wouldn't you expect eight years of fear and uncertainty to leave lines deep enough to sow runner beans? Not Cara. Had they found her son's body, of course, the story would be very different, but for eight years, she'd been hiding gut-wrenching terror. Imagine the vacuum of being unable to function, unable to plan, unable to grieve, unable to remember what laughter was like, or how it felt to run with the wind in your face. Every baby, every child, reminds you of Thomas. Every time you turn a corner you think, is that him? Manners and small talk were de rigueur in society — *I'd never have met the Gibson Girl in person* — *you're a long way from Oakbourne* — *in my opinion, they are better than the best* — but make no mistake, scratch the veneer and you find a mother whose only job is to be here when her baby comes home, so she must stay exactly the same as the day he left.

The mother Thomas would still recognise...

'Today —' Cara swallowed. Closed her eyes. Took a breath. 'Today, I don't even have that. Oh, I've stationed men at the gates and set up patrols of the grounds sure enough, but the press have no respect for property or privacy, and God knows, privacy is all that I ask.'

Julia glanced at the coachman who'd been tasked with making sure his mistress wasn't spotted under the pile of blankets as the brougham clopped through the journalists crowding the gate. Watched him move from polishing the harnesses to buffing an invisible mark on the door. Ribbons of mourning crêpe fluttered in the late summer breeze. The two black Friesian stallions snickered softly.

'You have no one to call for support?'

Cara looked away. 'I'm ashamed to say I do not.'

Julia laid a hand on her arm. 'You do now.'

'No, no. I couldn't possibly impose!'

'You're not. I'm simply offering moral support, if you'd like it.'

Relief seemed to make Cara's knees week. For the second time, Julia caught Cara as she tottered.

'I — would like that very much.' Cara's voice cracked. 'It's been a long time since … since I had a friend.'

'In which case, we'll do what friends do best. Send the vultures packing and make sure your privacy stays tighter than a loan shark's fist.'

Was that the ghost of a smile? 'You're very kind, Mrs. McAllister.'

'Julia. Call me Julia. Well, no, actually — call me any time. I mean that.'

In terms of morality, Julia felt neither pride nor shame. When your whole life is a lie, deception goes with the territory, though God knows it was the truth about knowing pain and loneliness in times of crisis. No one gathers friends and family round the table to share the experience of shooting their stepfather six times in cold blood, then burying his body in an unmarked grave.

Did Julia regret killing her stepfather? Not a pang. He was a monster, a brute, a bastard to his marrow, and if ever the devil walked this earth, it was him. What human would turn boots, belts and fists on a defenceless woman, reducing her jaw and cheek bones to splinters and beating a boy so badly that he'd never walk straight again? Assuming he could walk at all. Even so, there was a price to pay. There always is. Julia was barely fourteen at the time, and the pain of leaving the only two people she loved, knowing she'd never see either of them again, was indescribable then, and still was. On the other hand, they say the Irish have all the luck, but that wasn't true. Sam Whitmore rescued her, taught her the business, showed her there was light after darkness, and became not just a friend and mentor, but a second father on top.

Cara had no one.

Suddenly this was no longer a case of finding answers to questions, or saving Collingwood from himself. This was a fight for the truth, and for justice.

CHAPTER 7

'Come on, Charlie, give it to me straight. Am I dying or not?'
Standing at the window of his office in Boot Street,
Collingwood fumbled his notebook out of his pocket. 'See
this? My fingers aren't capable of flipping the bloody thing
open, much less writing notes. It's like having sausages tied to
hands that belong to somebody else, a steam hammer's trying
to blast my brains out through my ears, my shirt's soaked, plus
there's this vile, metallic taste in my mouth that no amount of
Constable Robbins' coffee can shift, and God knows that can
give disinfectant a run for its money.' He turned to his tall,
cadaverous sergeant. 'What do you reckon? Influenza?
Bronchitis? Pneumonia? Gall stones?'

Charlie Kincaid drew on his pipe, held the smoke for a while,
then let it out in a slow, upward plume. 'Worse, I'm afraid, sir.
Sobriety.'

'I am your superior officer, Charlie, and these are dire
symptoms. You'll have to come up with a diagnosis more grave
than a hangover.'

'The clap?'

'Very funny.'

'I thought so.'

For several minutes, both men stood at the window staring
down into the street, pretending to be engrossed in the butcher
gutting a pig.

'You are. You're going to poke that bear,' Kincaid rumbled
at last.

'There's a cat burglar working his way through our manor,
Charlie. It's my job to apprehend him.'

'In other words, yes. Despite the super's orders, you're hell bent on prodding the grizzly.'

'My sole priority is to catch a jewel thief, Sergeant, and I don't need to repeat what the super said about losing your job if you fail to toe the line.'

Charlie watched the butcher toss a scrap of liver to his dog. 'Two sticks are better than one when it comes to prodding.'

'Wrong. Any risks I run, I run alone.'

'With due respect, sir. Balls. If you go down, we all go down.'

Kincaid was right. For a while now, the Top Brass had been looking for an excuse to close Boot Street, open a bigger station with a broader jurisdiction and put a DCI in charge, one they could control. Like the army, they wanted discipline and lines, and disapproved of Collingwood's use of a so-called scene-of-crime photographer. They tolerated his enthusiasm for standardising mugshots, using twenty-four pre-set measurements from ears to hairlines to noses, to record and identify criminals, because of its effectiveness. And they were less suspicious than they used to be about his introduction of paraffin wax and resin compounds to preserve footprints at the scene, and dynamometers that could measure the amount of force used in breaking and entering. Even so, there was far too much French technology in play for their liking. What was he, some ruddy spy?

'I tracked down the Mile End Monster, Charlie, when I wasn't even in the Met, just drafted in to help.'

'That lot? They can't find their arses with their elbows.'

'Thank you for that vote of confidence, Sergeant.'

'What? No! I never meant it that way, and you bloody know it. *Sir.*' Kincaid tapped out his pipe on the windowsill, plugged in fresh tobacco and lit it. 'What I was trying to say, obviously badly, was that most coppers, or rather most detectives, stick to good old-fashioned groundwork, picking up leads and following 'em. You're different. More to the point, you think different.'

'Do I now.'

'For instance, you'll have a suspect in the cells, but instead of bashing him round the head, you don't utter a peep. You just sit back, fold your arms and let him think you know the answers, even when you don't.'

'Outwit them with silence, eh?'

'Silence makes a guilty man uncomfortable, and I've learned a lot from the way you let these felons dig deeper and deeper holes until they can't get out.' Kincaid grinned. 'In fact, my knuckles are most appreciative of your technique.'

'That wasn't how I caught the Mile End Monster.'

'If I recall, you studied the victims, the method of attack, the characteristics of both crime and criminal, the times and places where the women had been assaulted, then pieced together a pattern and caught him just before he violated another young girl in her bed.'

'Exactly how I plan to catch the jewel thief.'

'You made your name and reputation with that case, John. Don't undo all the good work by poking around in cases that don't concern you.'

'A child went missing.'

'I know.' Kincaid laid a hand on his shoulder. 'And you think that because you couldn't save your daughter, you can make it right by saving Cara Forbes.'

A lump formed in Collingwood's throat. 'What's wrong with that?' As a consequence of war, Kincaid had lost several friends, two fingers and his left ear. None of that hurt a fraction of what he was feeling now. 'What's wrong is if you *can't* find that kid.'

CHAPTER 8

Out in the fields, labourers were gathering blackberries, gooseberries, raspberries and a fruit that Forbes had only this year shipped over from California, a raspberry-blackberry hybrid called Logan's berry. Orchards throbbed with equal activity, as apples, plums, damsons and pears dropped into the baskets, while the leaves on the trees geared up to take on the furious colours of autumn.

Julia stretched out her legs in Cara's carriage, her bicycle secured with the luggage. Due to their compact size and popularity with doctors, the smaller models were nicknamed the pill box. It would have to be a bloody great tablet for this thing to qualify. Accommodating four people, and with glass windows, blankets, footstools and excellent suspension, this wasn't just travelling in style. This was luxury. It had curtains for privacy, two horses for speed, and the coachman wore the same livery as the plush blue interior. There was even the Forbes crest on the doors.

She let the late summer sun warm her face through the glass while the coachman navigated gentle hills softened by hedgerows and woodlands, past paddocks where horses flicked their tails in the shade of ancient, gnarled trees, and across streams that were a haven for wildlife. A blue spiral of bonfire smoke twisted up to the sky. Dandelion clocks and thistle seeds peppered the air. Red admiral butterflies, offspring of the spring migration, made their way south. Rabbits scampered into the undergrowth.

Perfection that not even murder could change, and perfection, as Julia discovered in the archives, was a quality where Austin Forbes refused to compromise. When the land belonged to the Davenport family, everything from onions to beetroots, rhubarb to cherries, were sold fresh at market, along with pasture lands, hayfields and livestock. Within a month of taking control, Austin turned three hundred years on its head. Arguing that too much fresh produce was going to waste, he decided to concentrate on fruit, and fruit alone, then turn the whole lot into conserves. Having already made his fortune in manufacturing and with an excellent railway link at hand, he set up jam production to his usual exacting standards, launching a range of such quality that almost immediately, and virtually without precedent, he was granted a Royal Warrant from the Queen.

Listening to the lunchtime chatter in the Bedford Hotel, opinion was divided. Some called Austin a visionary. Some called him a martinet. Most, of course, called him a bastard. Either way, it seemed Mr. Forbes didn't give a toss for anyone else's opinions. As far as he was concerned, that perfectionism produced some of the finest conserves in the business. Could a competitor have tried to level the field?

'We're approaching the bend, madam,' the coachman called down. 'Time to draw the curtains.'

Once through the gates and past the crush of reporters, Julia opened the curtains. Impressive wasn't the word. From the top of its slate roof to the bottom of its pillared entrance, Chislehurst Hall was architectural perfection. Not exactly overlooked either, she mused, as the brougham clopped up a quarter mile of gravel drive, and none too cramped inside from what she'd read. Three wings, fourteen bedrooms, stable blocks, not to mention its very own chapel. Topiaried box plants flanked an impressive oak doorway, marble statuary dotted the lawns, and the *parterre* looked like it was trimmed with nail-clippers twenty-four hours a day. How was it possible that the residents of such a composed and orderly residence had been a target for violence, not once, but twice over?

Yet for all its opulence, the overriding impression was that this was a fortress, rather than a home. That the place had been built to impress, rather than lived in.

'Madam.'

The butler, a heavyset cove in morning jacket and gloves, bowed to both women, before escorting them through a cavernous vestibule that boasted not one, but two spiral staircases, making it apparent that Chislehurst Hall extended even deeper than its imposing appearance led you to believe. Austin Forbes might be New Money, but with this house — these lands — he was trying to create history, and that's where New Money comes a cropper. Pedigree doesn't come out of a factory like a jar of strawberry jam, and from its heavy oak panelling to its dark, maroon drapes, the gloom she'd sensed earlier closed in like fog. The whole place reeked of trying too hard.

The staff in Chislehurst Hall walk on eggshells.

Did they? Listening to the two assistants in the haberdashery, Julia was willing to bet neither of them had ever set foot in this house. How often do assumptions become fact? Now, even though the house was in mourning, with every mirror draped with black crêpe, curtains drawn, lilies everywhere, she realised it was truth rather than gossip. Gliding like ghosts, the multitude of servants set to dusting, polishing, buffing the silver walked with their heads turned to the floor, not daring to make conversation in the cathedral-like hush.

'It was terribly good of you to drop everything and come like this,' whispered Cara, another downtrodden creature.

Engrossed with art in the style of Vermeer and van Dyck (was that a real Canaletto?) that lined the long corridor, not a speck of dust on their ornate frames, Julia had only just noticed that Cara's waist was nipped in so tight, it was a miracle the woman could breathe. Would that change, now Austin was no longer around to tell her how to dress? Or was she so institutionalised that she would still try to please a dead man?

'I can't tell you how much I appreciate your giving up your afternoon off,' Cara continued. 'It's been so long since I've been able to take tea in the Green Room, and having you here —'

'You don't need to explain, it's my pleasure.' *Classy ladies like her don't go round advertising their bruises.*

'You're obviously a very fashion-conscious young lady. Please borrow any hats of mine that you like. I'm sure you'll find something in my collection to suit, but my goodness, I'm getting ahead of myself.' Cara motioned for Julia to sit. 'Do, please, make yourself comfortable.'

That would be difficult. For one thing, the room wasn't so much a *salon* as a museum, and for another, Cara was so tightly strung, you could play Beethoven's violin concerto in D major on her back. In addition, whoever named it the Green Room was colour blind. Closer to grey. Grey like mould, Julia decided, perching on the edge of a Louis XV chair that was designed to be admired, rather than sat in.

'Bakewell tart?' Cara prompted, as the footman padded round with the cake stand, a pockmarked young man with slightly bucked teeth, whose tails sat too short on his gangly frame. 'Cook's shortbread melts in the mouth, and I can personally vouch for the smoked salmon sandwiches.'

Could she? Even allowing for modern corsetry, Cara's waist was tiny, her neck so slender, that Julia imagined wrens ate heartier meals. With her enviable figure and a face that revealed nothing of her traumatic past, Julia didn't see Cara staying a widow for long, but nibbling bite-sized apricot tarts and sipping lapsang souchong when her husband lay in the chapel smacked of a little girl's tea party with teddies and dolls. How long could Cara keep up the pretence? How long before she found herself facing reality? *Before she had to face losing Thomas twice over...?*

'Is everything all right?'

'I'm fine, dear.' Cara hugged her arms closer still to her body. 'It's just a little chilly today, don't you think?'

Grief does that. Makes you cold. Twelve years on, Julia still hadn't thawed out, and doubted the hollowness inside would fade. What made her heart twist, though — given that Forbes treated his workers like dogs, his servants like dirt, and his wife worse than the rest put together — was that Cara, poor bitch, was actually grieving.

You have no one to call for support?

I'm ashamed to say I do not.

Whether Austin physically beat her, or the abuse was purely emotional, Julia recognised this behaviour. Her mother had also been systematically bullied and belittled, isolated from her family and friends, leaving her vulnerable and alone until she was brainwashed into believing it was love.

'Absolutely,' Julia breezed. 'I felt a distinct hint of autumn this morning.'

Watching Cara cast nervous, darting glances at the window, even though the curtains were closed, Julia was reminded of the woman two doors down from the mining cottage where she grew up, on hearing how her nine-year-old daughter had fallen into the ore crusher and died. Julia was no more than six, but it was the first time she'd heard of anyone dying, leastways not someone she knew, and the neighbour's drawn face and blank eyes remained scorched in her memory. If she wasn't tugging at her neckline, she was pulling at her sleeves, as though trying to disappear inside her clothes. Exactly like Cara did now. In the corner, the pendulum from the grandfather clock had been removed, as befits mourning tradition. Somehow, though, she could still hear its ghost, ticking their lives away.

Tick, tock. Tick, tock. Tick, tock.

While the footman refilled her cup, Julia studied the ancestral portraits that had been so lovingly painted, though whose ancestors they were was a mystery. Not Austin's, that's for sure. He was a self-made man, though he had a taste for fine things, she'd give him that. Like the heavy panelling in the hall, it would not be her choice, but from the kidney-shaped satinwood desk inlaid with burgundy leather to the black lacquered chest with bronze doré trim, the ormolu ewers and rosewood pedestals, this room was crammed with antiques that had been crafted with passion. For all the exquisite marquetry and crystal chandeliers, though, the black lacquered Chinese screen and brocade footstools, there was still no warmth to this house.

Nothing to suggest that these walls had once echoed with laughter.

'Have you given any thought to what you'll do after the funeral?'

Wonder what'll happen to the business. No sons. No heirs. No nothing.

Can't see Mrs. F taking over.

'I can't stay here.' Cara leaned forward. 'Straight after —'

'There's a policeman to see you, Mrs. Forbes.'

Cara jumped like a startled rabbit, slopping tea in the saucer.

'A Detective Chief Inspector Dudley from the —'

'Show him in.' The cup rattled in its pool as Cara placed it back on the table. 'I don't know if this means they've made an arrest.' She shot Julia a haunted look. 'But you can't imagine what a comfort it is, your being here.'

Oh, but Julia could. She imagined only too well. The interval between death and burial is interminable as it is. A limbo of grief, disbelief, and unfinished business. Add on the torture of murder, the agony of a missing child, and the press swarming like ants, it was a wonder Cara's nerves could function at all.

'Comfort is my middle name,' Julia assured her, and while they waited for the policeman to be shown in, she reflected how the widow might have suddenly become an immensely rich woman, but it's a funny thing, wealth. Ask anyone in Broadhurst, London, the whole world in fact, and most people will say the same thing. They'd cut off their right arm and both legs to enjoy the kind of status and power that gives you the ability to buy anything, or anybody, you want, and never have to worry about paying a bill.

Tell them Cara's story. See how many would swap places then.

'You have the man who killed my husband, Chief Inspector?' Cara jumped up from her chair as he entered.

'We have a suspect.' Tall, stout and bearded, Dudley had a face like a gnarled tree, the voice of a diplomat and walked like he suffered from piles. 'The day before he died, Mr. Forbes dismissed his head book-keeper, Ezra Higgins. I presume you know about this?'

'Austin never discussed business with me. Though I am, of course, well acquainted with Mr. Higgins and his wife. They have a baby. A son.' Cara's features softened. 'Eight months old, I visit him regularly. Gave him a lovely little gown for his christening. Silk, trimmed with Valenciennes lace, and a sweet matching cap.'

'Quite so.' Dudley coughed. The subject of babies was clearly not a road he intended, much less wanted, to take. 'The thing is this. When he was at the bank on Monday, Mr. Forbes requested an inspection of his business account, where it immediately became apparent that the balance was three hundred pounds short.' He consulted his notes. 'According to the manager, the inspection was not something Mr. Forbes was in the habit of making, suggesting several weeks, possibly the end of the financial year, before the theft would be noticed.'

'Not Ezra, Chief Inspector.' Cara shook an emphatic head. 'He has worked for my husband for fifteen, sixteen years, and while I know nothing about book-keeping, I imagine any of the clerks with access to the accounts could have siphoned it off.'

'Three hundred pounds is an awful lot,' Julia chipped in. Six years' salary for the average labourer, and at least three for a book-keeper. 'I assume the Chief Inspector traced Mr. Higgins through his financial difficulties?'

'Funnily enough, no, Miss.' He eyed up her bloomer suit, contrasting the widow's mourning clothes with the frivolous green velvet, white ruffled blouse, white ankle boots and boater. 'We found no evidence of debt, or any suggestion that he was a gambling man, or involved in smuggling, or indeed any other illegal activities.'

'There you are. You have the wrong man,' Cara said.

'Quite possibly. Like I said, he's merely a suspect, but he does own a shotgun and one of his hobbies is shooting.'

'I assume, then, you've questioned every man in the area with a shotgun licence?'

'I appreciate your faith in the book-keeper, Mrs. Forbes, but your husband confronted Higgins in his house on Monday evening, where he found three hundred pounds in his sideboard, for which Higgins offered no explanation.'

'Where on earth did you get all this nonsense?'

'Your husband took his factory manager with him,' Dudley said patiently. 'It was he who showed us the money your husband had locked in his safe, to be paid into the bank on Tuesday morning before he died. He also told us how your husband dismissed Higgins on the spot, and served him with an eviction notice effective the end of this week.'

Desperate times call for desperate measures, Julia thought, *but a highly qualified, highly respected employee like Ezra didn't fit the "desperate" bill. Also, for a man with no debts and no shady dealings, he would have been well aware of the risk he was running, especially after the Christmas incident in which three workers and their families were thrown in the street. Unless…! Unless it wasn't a question of not expecting to get caught, more an intention to return the money once whatever crisis he was involved with was over.*

'Theft's a long way from murder,' she said.

'Exactly why we're keen to question him.' Dudley turned back to Cara. 'I will be frank with you, Mrs. Forbes. I have a list as long as my arm of men your husband bribed, duped or bullied to get what he wanted.' *Not so much a question of who'd want him dead. More who wouldn't.* 'But yesterday morning, Higgins left home, taking his shotgun with him, and has not been seen since.'

'Oh, dear God!' Cara clamped both hands over her mouth.

'I'm posting constables at the gate,' Dudley said. 'Realistically, he's unlikely to stroll up the main drive and knock, but if he does have any — let's say, funny ideas about extending his grievance, a heavy police presence ought to deter him.'

'You think —?' Cara cleared her throat. 'You honestly think I'm in danger?'

The diplomatic tones went into overdrive. 'I've served the police force for nearly forty years, Mrs. Forbes, and I still can't predict which way a man will turn when he's under duress. Folk bottle things up, until their idea of what it means to protect their family gets twisted out of all proportion. From then on, there's no reasoning with them.'

'In other words, I'm his next target?'

'We know Higgins is armed, it's fair to assume he is dangerous, but beyond that, your guess is as good as mine. Which is why I would like your permission to search every inch of Chislehurst Hall, the outbuildings and grounds.'

'Of course, Chief Inspector. You don't need to ask.'

'Thank you, and while I suggest you keep your doors locked at all times until we find him, I would also advise you not to worry. I've pulled my officers away from every other investigation, this case is top priority.' He shook hands. 'We'll soon flush this fox out of its hole.'

CHAPTER 9

In the velvety blackness, where crickets chirped in the grass and barn owls swooped on silent wings, a ladder was being propped against a wall. Stealthy feet climbed the rungs. An open window eased wider. Gently, so as not to wake anyone. The paws of the cat padded over the rug.

Antique furniture gleamed in the light of the moon. The walls shone with the oils from the paintings that covered them. There was no breeze to set the crystals in the chandelier tinkling.

The cat set to work.

A few minutes later, a jewellery box opened. Deft fingers searched through the necklaces, bracelets, diamonds and pearls until it found what it was after. A brooch in the shape of a dragonfly. Exquisite, rose-cut diamond wings. Ruby and diamond abdomen and thorax. Legs and antennae solid gold. Valuable, but not so precious that it needed to be locked up in a safe. Valued, but not worn so often that it would immediately stand out as missing.

The brooch slid inside a pocket.

The cat purred as it shinned down the ladder.

What the —? Julia rolled out of bed, lifted the sash and leaned out, her dark hair tumbling over the windowsill. Since when did half-blind, homeless soldiers start perching up stepladders, rubbing down rotten woodwork with horseshoe reeds and scrapers?

'Billy, stop.'

Those weren't her stepladders, and while dirty pictures could easily see a girl locked up, Julia was damned if she'd go down for receiving stolen goods.

'Can't hear yer. Must be dust in me ears.'

'Seriously, Billy. You have to stop now.'

'Yeah, yeah, nearly there. Two more panes and this frame's finished.'

'Your toast and eggs are burning.'

'Then why didn't yer say so!'

Electric bolts couldn't have shot him down faster, and if that grin was any wider, his lips would be meeting at the back of his head.

'This is about the bees, innit?' he said ten minutes later, after *he'd* made the coffee, and *he'd* made the toast, and *he'd* scrambled the eggs, and *he'd* fried the bacon, while Julia was pulling on a blouse and skirt, running a wet flannel over her face and taking a brush through the tangles.

'Are they nesting?'

'Who?'

'The bees. I presume they're under the roof, like the wasps that got in above the tailor's last —'

'Bees an' honey. Money.'

'Ah, well, that's the thing, Billy. If Mr. Whitmore had sufficient funds, the woodwork wouldn't have fallen into such a state —'

'S'all right, sweetheart, you don't have to pretend.' There it was, that sideways twinkle as he crunched on his toast. 'We both know it's just you on your tod, doin' the best yer can, woman in a man's world and all that. That's why I pitched in. I know what it's like, swimming wiv sharks.'

'Sharks?' Rhyming slang for larks? Marks? Parks?

'Big fishy things with sharp teef.'

Oh. Sharks. 'Well, I still don't have the mon— bees to pay you.'

'Yeah, I'd kinda noticed there's hardly a stick in the place. Even the dust motes echo when they land.'

Julia sighed. 'Long story.'

To quote Oscar Fingal O'Flaherty Wills Wilde, no good deed goes unpunished. With the law breathing down her neck so hard she could smell toothpaste, there had been no time to sell furniture. And since fugitives on the run rarely need an emergency gravy boat or a fallback canteen of cutlery, she'd given everything away.

'I'm not looking to be paid, luv. The way I see it, I got silver in the stars, gold in the sunset, and diamonds sparkling on the water, and I don't need dosh the same way most people do, Mrs. Mack.'

Con artists come in all shapes and sizes and Julia wasn't fooled by Mr. Briggs, but despite promising herself "no more waifs and strays", she enjoyed his company. All the more, perhaps, knowing he'd soon be moving on.

'Julia,' she corrected.

'Blimey, you feminists! Really are changing the way things work, aintcha? But like I says, you saw straight frew me and gave me a slap-up meal in spite of it. In my book, confidence on that scale deserves loyalty in return, and as you can see, I'm a dab hand at rubbin' down old wood.'

'On stolen stepladders.'

'Borrowed, if you don't mind. In fact, if it hadn't been for you draggin' me away, they'd be back behind the shed in the allotments by now.'

'I'm not letting you sleep here, Billy.'

'Don't want to, luv.' Either he was an exceptional actor, or he was genuinely surprised that she'd suggested such a thing. 'Got a nice little pitch down by the canal. Suits me very nice for the minute.'

'Until the grass needs inspecting in the next field?'

He stopped chewing. 'Summit like that.'

She'd touched a nerve, and wished she could take it back.

'So then.' Billy, being Billy though, bounced back straight away. 'Why the face like a wet wash rag?'

Clearly Julia wasn't the only one in this room who could read people. 'Couldn't sleep.'

More accurately, she didn't try. Immersing herself in stinky chemicals, surrounded by bottles and jars, hoses and jugs, dipping the negatives in the fixing bath and waiting for the images to form before sliding them into the wooden developing frame until four in the morning was the only way she could take her mind off a small boy snatched from his bed. Even if the photos were of his father's murder.

This was so unfair! Between Austin's dubious business dealings and his multitude of affairs, such a long list of suspects was thrown up that she'd expected the investigation to run long enough to find answers (by which she meant peace) for Cara.

Instead, it was over before it had started.

Julia's fork pushed the scrambled egg round her plate. Ezra had stolen such a large sum that a prison sentence was inevitable, and the factory manager stressed how Austin intended to visit the police station after paying the money back in the bank. What bothered Julia was that the two crimes didn't add up.

Embezzlement isn't exactly spur-of-the moment. In fact, it was so carefully thought out that Ezra clearly expected to get away with it, but being caught red-handed rarely tips mild-mannered clerks into murder. Was he so outraged that Austin was punishing his family for a crime they had nothing to do with that he sought revenge? More likely his intention was simply to scare his employer. Threaten him at the muzzle end of a shotgun into changing his mind.

Stubborn so-and-so, Old Man Forbes.

Never overturned a decision in his life.

Maybe Ezra's hands were shaking at the unfairness of it all, and his finger slipped? Maybe he was the one who'd tripped? Either way, once his victim was down, there was still a chance to make things right. Had Austin not been Austin…

Even bleeding like a hog, obstinacy prevailed, and the more he refused to apologise or back down, the more frustrated Ezra would have grown. This, remember, was a man who'd only ever wanted to look after his family. Turning them out wasn't right.

Boom!

Killer shot.

CHAPTER 10

'Good morning.' The voice was female, cultured, confident and melodic.

'A very good morning to you, too,' Julia replied.

Not everyone, it seemed, was put off by peeling paintwork. Or was it simply one of the china dogs in the window that caught this woman's eye? God knows, without those ugly little buggers selling at ridiculous profit margins, Julia couldn't keep her head above water. The only question, really: was this glamorous client a Pomeranian, or more of an Airedale?

'I would like to have my portrait taken.'

Head to toe in powder blue silk, she rustled when she crossed to shake hands, and quite frankly, Julia had never seen so many rare feathers and fine lace on one woman outside of royalty, with more frills on her parasol than you'd think would fit on. Better still, there were enough diamonds round her neck to make a jewel thief cough blood. Finally — finally! — a chance to pay off the butcher, because while Billy might be happy with gold in the sun, it was no substitute for coal in the winter.

'When did you have in mind?' Julia tried to make it sound as though her appointment book was full.

'Ideally right now, but if it's not convenient —'

'Now's fine.' Deep breath. 'Unfortunately, Mr. Whitmore's been called away, but these are all my work.' Julia made a broad sweeping gesture at the framed photographs on the wall. Weddings, babies, family groups, portraits, a few (fiercely romanticised) agricultural scenes, and some simply because the timing was perfect when it came to capturing mist in the valleys, ripples of raindrops or reflections on water. 'It goes without saying that if you're unhappy with the result, we can re-book for when my employer returns.'

'Correct me if I'm wrong, but isn't it you, rather than Mr. Whitmore, who undertakes commissions for the local police?'

'It is.'

'In that case.' She shot Julia a beaming smile. 'I promise to stay as still as the corpses you photograph at your murder scenes.'

'This way, Mrs —?'

'Davenport. Alexandra, but everyone calls me Lexie. Makes me feel so old and frumpy, otherwise.'

One thing this woman could never be accused of was frumpy! Leading her through to the studio, Julia was glad, more than ever, that the only reason she hadn't given away the fixtures and fittings in her shop was so people wouldn't know she'd skipped town. And by people, of course, she meant the police.

Her client wasn't young. Forty at a guess, with lines round her eyes that even expertly applied cosmetics couldn't hide, and there were streaks of silver in her caramel curls. Even so, Julia was certain these were the bluest, most disingenuous eyes she'd ever come across. Eyes, she calculated, that would photograph exceptionally well. Wait...

Did she just say Davenport? *As in Henry* —? The man who shot himself after assigning three hundred years of proud heritage to some Johnny-come-lately, leaving a wife and daughter to pick up the pieces?

'Is that why you want my services? Because I have the ear of the police?'

She expected Lexie to bridle and storm out. Instead, she let out a spontaneous laugh. 'You don't beat around bushes, do you?' Big, blue eyes surveyed the painted backdrops, ranging from park scenes to seasides to first class railway carriages. 'I'll be frank with you, Mrs —'

'Julia.'

'— when I read that piece in the *Oakbourne Chronicle*, where they'd had an anonymous tip-off about a cat burglar on the prowl, it unnerved me.'

In Julia's dictionary, unnerved meant what Cara was suffering. A stomach that wouldn't stop churning, a head that wouldn't stop pounding, bones that ached to the marrow and now, thanks to Ezra Higgins on the loose, the flight of owls became the whispers of ghosts. Was that the bark of a fox, or a cry of distress? Settlement creaks turned into gunshots.

'In which case,' Julia said levelly, 'you should report your concerns to the police.'

'I would, had their entire manpower not been diverted to the manhunt, which is why I was hoping you might know something about the thief's pattern of activities, to set my mind at rest.' Lexie peered behind the board painted with a terrace and balustrade. 'I'm sure you can appreciate how vulnerable three women, alone in a place as cavernous as Lindale Manor, might be feeling. Ah. This backdrop is perfect.' She tapped the giant wooden panel. 'What an absolutely charming Greek temple!'

Julia wondered how the vulnerable Lexie would feel if she knew that panel was hidden for a reason. And the only time it came out was to capture naked nymphs at play.

'I understand you're also a widow,' she was saying, as Julia lugged the backdrop into place. 'Do you mind my asking how your husband died?'

'Fighting in the Sudan.'

With luck, Lexie would attribute the sudden rush of colour to her cheeks as the result of exertion. Fingers crossed her own husband wasn't a casualty in the same campaign.

'Mine was killed at the Battle of Amoaful.'

Relief came out in a whistle, though if memory served, Amoaful was during the uprising on the Gold Coast of West Africa, after Britain bought the territory from the Dutch. Resentment that still simmered two decades on. 'You must have loved him very much,' Julia said, setting her camera on the tripod, 'not to have remarried.'

Lexie smiled. 'I suspect I'm preaching to the converted, but not every woman sees her destiny in terms of marriage, raising children, and staying at home with nothing but gossip and embroidery to amuse her.'

'Why should we?' Julia disconnected the hinge and gently unfolded the leather bellows. 'We're at the threshold of the twentieth century, and the walls of prejudice are crumbling fast. We have female doctors, female writers, female dentists, female scientists —'

'Female photographers.'

'Exactly. And one day, hopefully not too far off, we'll have the vote.'

It was no coincidence that the further technology advanced, the more independent women were becoming. Right now, despite the campaigns for suffrage that had been bubbling for the past thirty years, they still had no say in politics, though the outlook was improving. Women were routinely employed as book-keepers, telegraph operators, secretaries, nurses and clerks, with the bicycle offering them mobility and freedom like never before. Momentum in every sense of the word. Unfortunately, threshold of the twentieth century or not, this remained a man's world. Hence Julia's tissue of lies. But whichever way you stacked it, twenty years was a long time to stay single.

'Every night I drink a toast to feminine independence,' Lexie said, raising a pretend glass.

'Which is why, excuse my being blunt, you don't strike me as the type to be unnerved by a thief on the prowl.'

'It's precisely because I'm liberated that I'm worried.' Lexie swept up to the camera, bringing wafts of sandalwood, vanilla and patchouli with her. 'You live here in the centre of Oakbourne, surrounded by neighbours to help, and a police force to call on. It's very different when you live in the countryside, in a house that is isolated and exposed.'

'Surely you have staff?'

'Servants, not mercenaries. I can hardly ask them to arm themselves and keep watch through the night.' Lexie ran a gloved hand over the gleaming Spanish mahogany camera, tracing the dovetail joints with her finger. 'I'll be frank with you, Julia. After my father died, I went through a rough patch.'

'That has to be the understatement of the decade.'

'You mean my stepmother?'

Julia actually meant the rape of her lands, but sometimes you run with what you've been given. 'I read that the second Mrs. Davenport —' Lydia — 'is beautiful, elegant, and only four years older than yourself?'

'Classic gold-digger.'

'Except, as I heard it, she didn't inherit one damn thing in the end.'

He might have signed away vast acres of farmland for reasons he took to his grave, but Henry was landed gentry to his marrow. Lindale would pass through blood, not through marriage, and no matter what he might have intimated to Lydia, that manor was staying in the family.

'Gossip is invariably right, I've discovered. Under the terms of the will, she is entitled to live in Lindale until she re-marries or dies, but that is the extent of her inheritance.' *Perfect. A bitch of a stepmother you can't get rid of.* 'When he moved Lydia in, I moved myself and my daughter to the West Wing, after which the only contact I had with my father after that was through management of the estate.' Lexie's lips pursed. 'What people forget is, I didn't just lose my father that day. Our entire income dried up in an instant.'

A nice way of saying that his actions went way beyond anger, grief, shock and betrayal.

'At that point, Lydia and I had no choice other than to pull together, and it's funny. We were both braced to fight like cats in a sack. Instead we ended up liking each other.' Everyone expected her to sell up, she explained, but that was out of the question. 'Once upon a time, our walls dripped Constables, Gainsboroughs, even a small Tintoretto, and thick Turkish rugs covered the floors. Not these days.' She smiled. 'Which brings me to my point. Namely, that the few pieces of jewellery I didn't sell back then —' she tapped the diamonds round her neck and the swallow brooch at her breast, set with rose-cut diamonds and a cabochon ruby eye — 'are precious, but in sentimental, rather than financial terms.' Soft and round, even allowing for whalebones, that cleavage was not intended for celibacy. 'Now, if backstreet robbers stick a knife in someone's ribs out of frustration because they have no money, rings or timepiece to give them, imagine the reprisals a cat burglar might take, having ransacked the house and realised it's all been for nothing.'

'There's no suggestion the cat burglar is dangerous.'

'They said that about Ezra Higgins, and look how that turned out.'

Ah, yes. Julia wondered how long it would take to get round to Austin Forbes. 'If Ezra is indeed responsible,' she said smoothly.

For the first time, Lexie's act slipped. She recovered with commendable speed. But still. The mask slipped. 'In which case, the police are employing a great deal of manpower to track down an innocent man.'

'I wasn't suggesting he was innocent. Sit here, please.' Julia motioned her towards the marble bench — all right, wood painted white, but how many chaps, drooling over flip books of girls taking their clothes off or caressing one another, are going to notice what the bloody thing's made of? 'Now hold the parasol at an angle slightly to your left.' Perfect contrast to linear columns.

'What were you suggesting?'

Julia placed a bowl of fresh flowers next to the bench to balance the composition. 'It strikes me that there's more behind the embezzlement than —'

'The official line that's being thrown out?' Lexie's blue eyes danced. 'Don't tell me our illustrious pioneering crime scene photographer is a cynic who doesn't trust the police to do their job?'

'They made a poor fist of finding Baby Forbes.'

'Not for the want of trying.'

'And now the boy's father is dead.'

'Do…' The parasol was spinning so fast, the frills blurred and the breeze they whipped up made the props in the studio rattle. 'Do the police think Austin's murder and his son's kidnap are linked?'

Julia disappeared under the cloth to line up the shot. After all these years, she still felt a frisson of excitement at seeing the world upside down, and now, looking at this elegant creature fishing for information, a spark of mischief ran through her. 'They haven't ruled it out.'

The parasol shot through Lexie's fingers, sending roses and water over the floor. 'I'm so, so sorry. How clumsy of me. Thank goodness the vase didn't break.' She bent down to pick up the flowers, while Julia reached for a cloth to mop up. With luck, the shawl would have dried out by the time it came to covering Aphrodite's modesty and cavorting nymphs' blushes. If not … well, men do enjoy the sight of girls in wet garments. Those beach scenes weren't here for nothing.

'So then.' Lexie cleared her throat. 'The police think Ezra kidnapped Thomas, but something went wrong, resulting in the boy's death, which is why he didn't collect the money, and now, eight years later, someone found out, blackmailed Mr. Higgins, only Austin discovered the theft and Higgins killed him, then went on the run?'

Now that, Julia mused, wasn't the sort of supposition a person comes up with in the space of ten seconds. 'That's one theory.'

'It makes sense.' Lexie repositioned herself on the seat, fluffing up silks and feathers with her customary disingenuity. 'Eight years ago, he did something terrible, but having got away with it, he rebuilt his life. He took a young wife. Started a family. One can only imagine his shock when Austin discovered the shortfall, sacked and evicted the man who robbed and betrayed him, and that's the whole crux of crimes like this, isn't it? Men like Mr. Higgins still feel they've been wronged. That it's always someone else's fault, never theirs.'

The bigger the chip on a man's shoulder, the more extreme the lengths he'll go to to exact his revenge. 'Ezra can hardly play the injustice card here,' Julia said. 'He was caught pretty much with his fingers in the till.'

'How often is the fire of prejudice quenched by the water of logic?'

Too true. Every year, hundreds of lovers were murdered by jealous husbands. Not, you notice, their adulterous wives. No, it was invariably the poor sods who happened to be in the wrong place, at the wrong time, and had done nothing wrong. Fair or not, there was little justice when it came to passion.

Julia inserted the glass plate and slid the cover from its holder. 'It takes a very particular disposition,' she chose her words carefully, 'to drop a man with a single round, then calmly walk up and empty the second barrel at point blank range into his back.'

'Maybe Ezra was too scared of Austin to face him? Or — or — believed the first blast would kill him?'

'I dare say Chief Inspector Dudley will be asking the same questions, once he has his man in handcuffs.' Julia pressed the shutter release, changed the plate, took another, then another, then another. 'There now. All finished! Would you like to pick a frame? Ah, the silver filigree with the cherub in the corner. Good choice.' An interesting choice, anyway. Was it word association that made her choose a frame with a baby? Or something deeper, and infinitely darker?

'Thank you so much for fitting me in at short notice. When should I come to collect the portrait?'

'If you give me your number, I'll telephone.'

'We — don't have one.' Lexie made an expansive gesture with her hands. 'All this modern fandango, who needs it!'

Who can't afford it, more like.

The bell above the door tinkled when Lexie opened it to leave. 'If you post it, do remember I changed my name back to Davenport after my father died.'

'That was a bold move.'

'Not really. Austin Forbes set out to destroy us, and I was damned if was going to let him run us out of town, like some ruffian outlaws of the Wild West. Reverting to my maiden name was the first shot in my war of impendence.' Lexie stepped backwards into the street with a rustle of silk, pushed up her parasol and twirled it over her shoulder. 'And it is precisely because I am standing firmly on my own two feet that I worry about this cat burglar.'

'You shouldn't. The police are swarming like ants over your neck of the woods.'

'At the moment, but Mr. Higgins is hardly a seasoned criminal. It won't take long to round him up, and I don't know about you, but if I was a burglar, I'd say one of the softest targets is the house the police move away from.'

'Possibly, but — hey, look out!'

With a shriek, Lexie jumped clear as a gasoline-powered Benz tricycle spluttered down the thoroughfare. 'Oh my gosh, thank you!' She brushed her skirts, pushed a rebellious caramel curl back into place. 'Not simply for saving my life there, but for listening. I'm not saying my mind is at rest, but at least I have a clearer picture, thanks to you.'

'If I saved anything, it was a few mucky marks on your dress and perhaps the odd bruise. Those beasts are equipped with brakes, you know.'

'It appears that particular model comes equipped with a very loud horn and a wide range of swear words.' Lexie held out her hand for a farewell shake. 'Maybe you didn't save my life, Julia, but you saved my dignity, and for a woman that's even more precious.'

Once again, Julia begged to differ. Leaning her shoulder against the door jamb, she watched Alexandra Davenport cross the road before being swallowed up by the crowd and the traffic. The morning sun was pleasantly warm on her face, and on the Common over the road, small children chuckled and squealed.

Dignity, she mused, can never be taken. Bending down, she picked something off the pavement and held it in the palm of her hand. Dignity can only be surrendered, and when it comes to white flags, diamond swallow brooches were pretty damn conclusive.

Trick of the sun? Or did that cabochon ruby eye really wink?

CHAPTER 11

'Thanks for meeting me on neutral territory,' Collingwood said.

'I didn't realise we were at war,' Julia replied.

He almost smiled. 'I meant a place a detective inspector might go that wouldn't arouse the suspicions of his chief superintendent.' He held the door open for Julia. 'Taking a lady to lunch in a genteel tea shop fits the bill rather nicely.' Opposite a Russian watch-maker's and next door to a gallery running an exhibition of *art nouveau* oils, this was more than a tea shop.

With Broadhurst, it was a straight case of haves versus have-nots, where "those who had" had it in spades. The difference with Oakbourne was that it had evolved slowly, from medieval market town to modern industrial giant, with a class structure that ranged from the thousands of underprivileged factory workers to the middle classes of doctors, solicitors, bank managers and up, via an army of clerical staff, whose job was to ensure that the wheels of business ran smoothly. All of it interspersed with the commerce from the watery ribbon that bisected the town, the Southolt arm of the Grand Union Canal. But while Oakbourne's theatre couldn't compete with its neighbour's, and the music halls were nowhere near as opulent, the new glass arcade and explosion of galleries, jewellers, bespoke tailors and fine restaurants were giving it a bloody good run for its money.

'This way, sir, madam.'

The waitress, in a cap so stiffly starched that it could cross the Atlantic without sinking, steered them through clouds of customised fragrances and eddies of muted conversations to a circular table balanced on perilously pointed legs and laid with

Minton porcelain. The frames of the chairs were so highly gilded, Julia's eyes watered, and the seats were upholstered in a purple velvet identical in colour to the grapes on the swirling vine patterns on the floor. Mind you, would one expect anything less in an establishment like this? And don't even mention the soaring fluted columns and sculpted arches!

'Are you going to tell me what that shifty looking chap is doing outside your studio?'

If you didn't know better, you'd think the waters of Detective Inspector Collingwood's life were running smoothly. Grey worsted lounge suit, with creases in his trousers sharp enough to slice bread, matching Derby, high collar and spotted silk tie. He was close shaven now, smelling of his trademark *Hammam Bouquet*, inspired by Eastern harems, sultry steam baths, and boudoirs oozing sultans and sex. In fact the only thing missing was a cane to swing and he'd make a textbook Burlington Bertie from Bow. The perfect image, carefully cultivated to earn the respect of honest citizens bridging every stratum of society, yet at the same time urbane enough to coax details from witnesses, confidences from informants, and trick felons into thinking they were smarter than this posh twit in a fancy suit.

Julia, of course, did know better. 'You mean the poor, half-blind, homeless soldier rubbing down my paintwork?'

'Vagrancy's a crime.'

'That's all right, he isn't a soldier either.'

'You know he intends to rob you blind?'

'Won't he be in for a disappointment.'

Collingwood pulled his chair close to the table, leaned forward and lowered his voice. 'Look, I'm really sorry about Tuesday night.'

She thought back to the rap-tap-tap on her window. At the dishevelled creature outside. To placing a cold cloth on his forehead to ease his headache. Running him a hot bath. Sponging his back, soaping his hair, listening while he relayed his recent conversation with the chief superintendent. Leading him, naked, into her bed.

'It happens to every man once in a while, John.'

'Not to me, it doesn't!'

'There's nothing to apologise for, and nothing to be ashamed of.'

In an ideal world, the waitress wouldn't have chosen this particular moment to set down two bowls of potted shrimp and a basket of warm, crusty bread. What took two minutes felt like two hours.

'It was the first time we'd rumpled my sheets since your daughter died,' Julia said, once they were alone with their shrimps, 'and these are emotional times, John.'

She hadn't attended Alice's funeral. Not out of respect for a wife who hadn't allowed her husband in her bed since their honeymoon. It was graveyards. Too many people she loved had been claimed by that cold, hard, merciless clay.

'I don't think I'd quite sobered up,' he said sheepishly.

'I'm not quite sure you have now.'

No smile. Not so much as a twitch. 'It won't happen again, you have my word.'

She scooped up a thick, buttery shrimp on her spoon. If she'd had half the sense she was born with, she'd have stopped "it" before "it" even started. He was broken and in pain, he needed to heal, but suddenly there was the press of his lips, still wet from the bath — the glide of expert fingers — the urgency of his tongue exploring inside and out —

She cleared her throat. 'Every man cries at some point in their lives, John.'

'At the risk of repeating myself, *I* don't.'

She wanted to explain that it wasn't weakness. That he hadn't just been distraught at the manner of his daughter's death, he'd been furious. Raging at his wife, the world, himself most of all, to the extent that he'd lost perspective. As a father, he'd argued, his only job — his sole duty — had been to protect her, and what had he done? He had failed her. A child. A sick child at that. And he'd failed her. No amount of logic, not from Julia, the doctors, his colleagues, his friends, could make him see sense, and angles only skew further when seen through a bottle. He didn't cry when Alice died, he didn't cry at her funeral, or when he sold his house to pay for a "good" asylum for his wife, and there's only so long you can run before reality catches up. On Tuesday night, they'd both needed release, oh God, how they'd needed release, clawing at one another like animals in the dark. But with release came the liberation of pent-up emotion. In time, he'd come to see this was as inevitable as it was natural. Chinking china cups in fancy tea rooms wasn't that time.

'These are the crime scene photographs you asked for.' She passed the envelope across. 'You might want to finish your shrimps first.'

'Hm.' In a public space, and with a table by the window, he didn't take them out, merely peered inside and leafed through. 'I've seen worse.' He paused. 'But not often.'

Outside, on the pavement, a small boy rolled his hoop while his nanny chatted to a nursemaid rocking a pram. On the other side of the street was a purveyor of fine leather goods, a baker's, and a bookshop specialising in bibles. It felt strange to see the world looking so normal, because no matter how bad

Austin Forbes' faults may have been, no one deserved to die like that.

'Perhaps you'd give us ten minutes before bringing the main course?' he asked the waitress.

The way she blushed suggested she'd give him anything.

'It was you, wasn't it?' Julia said. 'That anonymous tip-off to the *Chronicle* about the cat burglar?'

Collingwood leaned back and draped his arm over the chair. 'Now why would a detective inspector do a thing like that, rather than release a formal statement?'

'Because he wants to force the thief's hand, and an official police interview, outlining the nature of the crime, might send him to ground. Whereas —' she fixed her gaze on the baker across the road, tray of hot loaves balanced on his head, his white apron in stark contrast to his red cheeks from the oven's ferocious heat — 'a tip-off about "paltry hauls", "lack of flair", and, oh dear, oh dear, "cowardice" is likely to have the opposite effect.'

She watched the baker stack the bread in his shop window. Big, fat 2lb. loaves in the middle, the sort that set a farm labourer back a quarter of his daily wages, ale bread on the left, crusty cottage loaves on the right. The rest he piled into the basket on his delivery boy's back, ready to be touted door-to-door round the streets.

'Do you think he'll take the bait?' she asked.

'Criminals are criminals the world over, Julia. They think they're clever, they convinced they're smarter than the police and won't get caught, but the one thing they can't abide, not under any circumstances, is to be seen as amateurs and viewed with contempt.'

'Especially when that derision is plastered over the front page of the *Chronicle*.'

'I'm betting that piece made him angry, and when a man gets angry, he gets reckless, and reckless leads to mistakes.'

'The cat becomes the mouse?'

'If I'm right, he'll squeak tonight, and the odds are he'll pick a house in Broadhurst, because New Money likes nothing better than to flaunt its wealth, and the more ostentatious the house, the higher the two fingers Puss can stick up to the press.'

They paused while the waitress set down Julia's ham omelette and Collingwood's mutton chop with carrots.

'Y'know, for a minute there, I could have sworn you said Broadhurst.'

'Can I help it if my job leads me to contact Chief Inspector Dudley?'

'It would be irresponsible to close the case before you confirm it's the same thief.'

'And as I'm leaving, it might also occur to be me to flatter some young constable into showing me the kidnap files from eight years ago.'

'In which case —' she couldn't keep the excitement out of her voice — 'I might have a lead for you.' She gave him the gist of Lexie's visit, emphasising how she couldn't have been quicker off the mark to seek out the police photographer, considering the piece about the cat burglar had only made the morning edition, and in the *Oakbourne Chronicle* at that. 'Not even Broadhurst!' Suggesting Lexie had been looking for an excuse, any excuse, to pick her police photographer brains. 'She made no attempt to disguise the bad blood between herself and Austin, but in her bid to win my friendship and trust, she let slip far too many confidences and gave me, someone she'd never met before, so much detail that it had the opposite effect. In fact, she was so desperate to know what action the police are taking that she overplayed her hand.' She showed him the little swallow brooch. 'She wants at least one more chance to suck me dry.'

Collingwood beckoned the waitress across and settled the bill. 'Your conclusion, Sherlock?'

'Elementary, my dear Watson.' Julia smoothed her skirts. 'Lexie Davenport is in it up to her neck.'

CHAPTER 12

Originally a fortified tower dating from Tudor times, Lindale Manor was about as imposing a building that Julia had ever seen. Lexie was right to fight to retain it. Its classic red brickwork, stepped gables and soaring chimney stacks were her birthright, which made it her daughter's — Henry's granddaughter's — birthright, as well. Julia wondered how far she'd go to protect it.

'Be careful,' Collingwood said, when she announced her intention to take Lexie's bait and return the little swallow brooch to its owner. 'Higgins is still out there. He'll be hungry, he'll be scared, he'll be jumpy, but most of all he'll be cornered.'

'I believe the expression you're looking for is trigger-happy.'

'Just be careful, Julia. Please?' He tipped his hat. 'The paperwork from losing my crime scene photographer doesn't bear thinking about.'

Comments like that, a man's lucky to walk away without a permanent limp, but policemen do have their uses. If you want to find out about someone, forget talking to their friends. Or their enemies, come to that. The source needs to be completely objective, without axes to grind or rose-tinted glasses, and Collingwood reckoned she could do worse than pay a call on the head gardener, now retired and living with his postmaster son, just round the corner from where they'd had lunch.

'He should be able to fill in some of the gaps. Just don't tell him I sent you.'

'Of course.' Julia tapped her nose and winked. 'You're off the case.'

'I arrested his grandson for drunk and disorderly.'

Far from finding an old man slumped in an easy chair, reading the paper and smoking a pipe, Aloysius Ingram Norris McNab — Joe to his friends — had a different slant on retirement. Arthritis might have curtailed any full-time gardening, but it didn't stop him giving his allotment patch hell. Better yet, he took talkative to an entirely new level.

'Not half,' he said, when asked if he missed the Manor. 'If it weren't for me hips, I'd still be there. Specially since it was me what designed the botanical gardens.'

Ah. Shame. For all him sowing his cabbages, lifting his carrots, ripening his marrows and dividing his chives with more gusto than men half his age, the poor old boy turned out to be senile. 'Austin annexed all the Davenport lands,' Julia pointed out gently.

'Ah, well, that's the thing.' Rake, rake, hoe, hoe. 'Mr. Henry only signed away those fields that was fertile and rich.' His spade hit the chives with unexpected ferocity. 'That's where I came in, see. As far as Miss Lexie was concerned, the few neglected acres and clogged pond that Forbes didn't want represented a lot more than people gave 'em credit for. In her mind, those grounds had cupped Lindale like hands for three hundred years. Now was her turn to protect them.'

More likely Miss Lexie's chance to put one over on Austin by showing the world that breeding triumphs over greed, Julia thought. Making him look small was her revenge.

'Three weeks after Mr. Henry's funeral, she hired me to turn those run-down plots into fully fledged botanical gardens. Fair jumped at the chance, didn't I? Drew up the plans, ordered the plants, then set about dividing the grounds into themed areas, she calls 'em rooms, and you have to hand it to her. She has vision, that woman.' The old man shook the dirt off a line of carrots and laid them in the barrow. ''Took a small army, but all that clipping and mowing, digging and dredging paid off. I've never seen a rose garden like it, not for its size. Riot of perfume right through the season. Topiaries are starting to come into their own. The ornamental lake is a dream.'

'How come no one's ever heard about this?'

'Not finished, is it? She's a right perfectionist, that one.' Said by a man with not a single weed in his allotment. 'Once it's fit for public viewing, that's when she'll announce it. Magnificent botanical gardens for people to enjoy for free —'

'Free?'

'Her attitude is that just 'cause folk don't get a chance to visit the likes of Kew don't mean they shouldn't have access to, her words: *an oasis of beauty, serenity, colour and joy.* An escape from the grinding misery of poverty any time they want, she reckons. Relief from the smog and dirt, and the relentless noise of the factories, and that's something else. Not afraid of getting her hands dirty, her. Morning till night, you'd see her planting, pruning, pulling up pondweed. Smell this.' He stuffed a sack under Julia's nose. 'Pretty rife, eh? Don't stop Miss Lexie. She's out there, spreading blood, fish and bone round her plants like it was stardust. Like everything else, mind, you get used to the pong after a while.'

'A hundred years and I'd still be gagging.' Julia was pretty sure her sinuses had melted. 'Nothing would ever encourage me get personal with that stuff, especially with an army of gardeners to call on.'

'Except she don't have 'em any more, does she? That all tailed off when she brought the handyman in, bit like the staff in that respect. By the time I left, she'd dismissed that many, I'd take my break not knowing whether I was seeing shadows, ghosts, or one of the few servants she'd kept on.' He took off his cap and wiped his brow. 'She knows how to pick 'em, mind. Clever lad, that Dickon Tyler. Done wonders patching the roof, laid new parquet in the dining hall, even replaced the panels in the ceiling where they collapsed. In fact —' the old man screwed up his face — 'come to think of it, I can't recall him tackling a single project that hasn't turned out well.'

'This might seem an odd question,' she asked Joe, 'but I don't suppose you know anything about that business when Austin Forbes sacked three men on Christmas Eve and —'

'*DO* I know about it!' Joe seemed tickled that she'd asked. 'Big, big story up at Lindale, that was. In fact, anything to do with Mr. Austin is headline attention up there, even though those three blokes had been trouble from the start.'

What kicked off this particular incident, he explained, was that their wives had been laid off since October, which was standard practice in the jam-making industry, but the men felt compelled to demand financial compensation for the inconvenience.

'Gotta have some degree of sympathy,' Joe said, watering his seedlings. 'It's barely subsistence wage for those girls, for which they're lugging heavy pallets of jars across the factory floor day in, day out, lifting half-hundredweight pans, and washing jars in fifteen-hour shifts.'

All the while, Julia mused, facing the constant threat of burns from open vats of bubbling fruit, or else from the clouds of steam rising from the scalding water in the exhaust pit.

'Which leaves 'em scratching round for charring and such in the slack season,' Joe said. 'It's no picnic, I tell you. Trouble was, them three girls ain't the only workers in the jam place, and their husbands was well known in certain public houses for shooting their mouths off. You can guess where this is leading, can't you?'

'Slack season. Drinkers. Let me guess, they'd fallen behind in their rent?'

'Bang on the nail, and that wasn't the first time they'd stirred up trouble, neither. The timing was unfortunate, I grant you, but —' Joe shot her a sharp glance over his watering can — 'Christian charity were never Mr. Austin's strong point.'

'You can say that again. He put one of the men in hospital for the New Year and beyond.' If that's how he reacted in public, what went on *inside* Chislehurst Hall? What, in God's name, did he do to Cara?

'The way I heard it, the drunken idiot swung a punch at Mr. Austin, Mr. Austin took a swing back, the boy ducked, it was icy, he hit his head as he fell, and you know doctors. Get into a right old spin when it comes to swellings on the brain. Kept him in, just to be sure's what I heard.'

'He could hardly afford a hospital bill, when he was already behind on the rent.'

'Mr. Austin covered it.'

'Guilty conscience? Or a pay-off?'

'Ah. Well. The only person who can tell you that is answering to a higher authority.' The old man tested the stakes on his runner beans. 'Daresay Mr. Austin could have handled it better, but he never did anything by halves, him, and them earlier tragedies would have hardened him up. Right through, though, Mr. Austin had the support of every businessman in the town, since they all think the same way. Anyone unhappy with working conditions is welcome to seek employment elsewhere.'

Wait, wait, wait. 'What earlier tragedies?'

'You don't know?' Bony hands closed round the handle of the spade until his knuckles went white. 'Well, then, if you have a spare moment, I suggest you take a walk round St. Michael's. You'll find all the answers you need there.'

Which is how Julia came to be staring at the imposing gables of Lindale Manor for several minutes.

Before pedalling past the gates in the direction of Broadhurst.

Graveyards weren't intended to be lonely places. They were meant to embrace the occupants in a communal hug, within both the physical and spiritual shelter of the church. Bollocks to that. These places made her skin crawl and caused her stomach to cramp. In fact, Julia dreaded even passing one, they stirred up the worst kind of memories.

The miners carrying her father's coffin on their shoulders.

The single red rose dropped into the pauper's graves of her models, slaughtered purely so some twisted fiend could frame her for their murders.

Sam, who'd saved her, loved her, taught her everything she knew, before the soil swallowed him forever.

And, worst of all and the most recent, the stone that was surely too heavy for the chirpy soul who lay underneath...

Julia blew her nose. Reminded herself that this wasn't about her, that she was here to do a job, so bloody well get on with it. Then pushed her shoulders back and strode down the path, trying to pretend this was another photographic shoot, and what a splendid picture it would make, the sun slanting through the ancient dense, dark yew trees.

The Forbes vault was easy to find. Built like a miniature classical temple from fine, white Greek marble, the pediment of the vault had been carved with a unicorn, symbol of courage. The black metal door was flanked by weeping stone angels, while clipped laurels stood guard on either side.

Grandeur which congealed into nothingness once you read the plaques.

Darling Sophie
Born June 5th, 1868
Died July 18th, 1868
Only a mother's love

And underneath:

Arabella
Born March 21st, 1871
Died March 21st, 1871
Safe in His arms

Holy mother of God.
No wonder the angels were weeping.

CHAPTER 13

In the slums, the towns, the cities, yes, Julia could easily imagine one human being staring down the barrel of a gun and shooting another in cold blood. But out here? Where kestrels hovered over the fields, hares bounded between the neat rows of currants, and butterflies flittered like multi-coloured confetti? Gone were the days when highwaymen roamed the countryside, yet for all the ducks shaking their feathers and swallows gathering in flocks, one human being had watched another make a tourniquet, then wriggle out of his frock coat to wrap the wound. Waited, while he crawled and hauled his way to his horse. Then, before he could reach it, coolly emptied the gun.

He'll be hungry, he'll be scared, he'll be jumpy, but most of all he'll be cornered.

Cycling past thatched barns and brick farmhouses, towering haystacks and tiled watermills, Julia knew Ezra Higgins could be nurturing his grievance behind any one of them, and fear made her whole body shake. Why put herself through this? Why deliberately lay herself open to danger? Desperate men often take hostages, and few of those hostages walk away. Why not turn the hell back, and leave it to the chief superintendent and DCI Dudley?

I slipped on the path, lovey, that's all.

Clumsy old me, tripped over the coal bucket.

Who put that door there, eh?

God knows, they were rough, tough men in the tin mines, her father included, but none of them were bullies or sadists. As a child, Julia couldn't understand why any person would take fists, feet and belts to a woman cowering on the floor, or hurt a little girl by strangling her kitten with unspeakable slowness. By the time comprehension dawned, it was too late. Her mother was disfigured and her brother was crippled, possibly for life. Child or not, she should have stepped in a long time before she finally put that monster in the ground, so come on, Ezra. Take your shot.

Julia had let her family down.

She would die before she let Cara down, too…

'Julia!' Lexie was standing in those transformed run-down acres, clipboard and pencil in hand, when Julia cycled up the drive. She had changed out of the powder blue silk into a plum-coloured day dress which, strangely for a woman with no man in her life, accentuated the swell of her breasts even more than the blue, though she still wore gloves. This time white lace. 'I didn't realise photographs could be developed so quickly!'

With no hat to hide them, the full extent of her jumbled caramel curls was apparent. Purple brought out the blue of her eyes. Why such sensuality, Lexie? 'Technology hasn't advanced that far, I'm afraid.' Julia reached into her reticule. 'I came to return this.' She passed across the diamond swallow in flight, set with a cabochon ruby eye.

'Oh my goodness!' Lexie pinned it to her dress. 'Thank you, thank you, thank you, you're an angel. It means so much, this piece, I truly thought I had lost it! But really. You didn't need to trail all the way out here to return it.'

'You didn't need to drop it at my feet.'

'I think you'll find it fell off when I had that altercation with the automobile.'

'I think you'll find clasps of this quality don't fall off unaided.'

At least Lexie had the grace to blush. 'You're not an easy woman to fool.'

'Then I suggest you stop trying.'

Besides, "all the way out here" wasn't actually that far. Studying the Ordnance Survey map, Julia was astonished to see that Lindale Manor was closer to Oakbourne than Broadhurst. A lot closer, in fact. Almost bordering the beauty spot where Austin was killed.

Someone had goaded a mild-mannered book-keeper into becoming a cold-blooded assassin. A coward, she'd decided, too gutless to pull the trigger themselves, and who fitted that bill better than three vengeful drunks with a chip on their shoulder, whose families were also thrown out on the spot? Brothers in arms in every sense. But now, fresh from the churchyard of St. Michael's, Julia was convinced the chip sat on an altogether more sensual shoulder.

'What do you think of my gardens?'

'They're beautiful.' Hell, no. They were stunning. A series of themed collections — rooms, Joe said she called them — showcasing plants and trees from every corner of the world, some separated by the original three-hundred-year-old walls, others by hedges, some by nothing more than raised walkways.

'That patch of rough ground is destined to become the Japanese garden. You can see the hole for the pond, there'll be weigela here, a flowering quince over there, I've ordered little red maples to dot here, here, and here, and in time I'd like to add a miniature tea house. Something for children to explore, allowing them to play and learn at the same time.' Lexie motioned for her visitor to pass through an arch of laburnum heavy with seed pods. 'This is the Himalayan room. As you can see, the bamboo orchids were a total disaster, ditto those poor ginger lilies, but if I replant with rhododendrons, it'll make a nice splash of colour in spring. My original intention was to keep the area to your left as a winter garden — oh, you should see the snowdrops, Julia! A sea of white, and for anyone who thinks they have no scent, all I say is, take a deep breath when they're in bloom. Light, fresh, with a slight hint of honey. It's amazing.'

Julia thought of the scents of sandalwood, vanilla and patchouli that Lexie had brought with her to the studio. The same scents that were wafting across now.

'Then I thought, no. Let's honour the men who lost their lives in the Crimea, so my next job is to plant the seeds which I've had shipped over. Grasses, mostly, with a sprinkling of pasque flowers, poppies and periwinkles. I'm hoping the sacrifice of others is something the poor and underprivileged will relate to.' Lexie smiled. 'My kitchen garden will probably be picked clean, but it's a small price to pay.'

'What's that?' Julia pointed to what looked like the crenulations of a medieval castle poking through the treetops.

Lexie's blue eyes flickered, the smile froze, and if Julia hadn't been paying close attention, she'd have missed it, the change was so fleeting. 'The folly. Don't you think the dahlias in the walled garden are just splendid? They're native to Mexico, but such natural hybrids, they really come into their own this time of year. My favourite is this little pink...'

Julia stopped listening. Once again, Lexie had overplayed her hand, twittering on about tubers as a distraction from what had, suddenly, become a very real focus of interest.

That folly was where the ransom had been left.

'...we still have the open grounds to the rear of the Manor to plan. So far, I've kept the landscape simplistic, with topiaries, rose beds and a small ornamental lake, though in time, if the gardens prove as popular as I hope, I'll incorporate a small maze for the children.'

Left, but never collected. 'When do you plan to open the gardens?'

'Many of the shrubs still need to establish themselves, but my fingers are crossed for next spring. Sadly, patience does not list itself as one of my virtues, so realistically it'll most likely be summer. By the way, I haven't seen the afternoon paper —'

Aha. Wondered how long it would take you to get round to it.

'— but I assume the police have arrested Ezra Higgins?'

'Why would you think that?'

Lexie stopped so abruptly that Julia almost cannoned into her. 'They haven't found him?'

'Not for the want of trying.' According to Collingwood, they'd checked the railways, the canals, every road, every bridge, every barn, every storehouse, not to mention every square inch of Forbes' property, from house to factory to warehouses, right down to the last jar of jam. 'As manhunts go, it's almost unprecedented.'

But only almost. Baby Thomas saw to that. Julia concentrated on the bees humming round the lavender and the perfume of the roses, still spectacular despite the lateness of the season. And tried not to think about a small boy whisked from his crib in the night.

'I expect he hitched a ride on the first train out of Broadhurst,' Lexie said.

'Possibly.' The search certainly bore out that theory. 'But most criminals hide out in familiar territory, and the police believe that, if this is the case here, he'll want to keep a close eye on his family.'

'Yes, I — ah, this is the kitchen garden I was talking about. Right now, we're using wood to divide the sections, but box plants would look softer, don't you think? Perhaps if I called it the Monastery Garden, it would put people off helping themselves —'

'What was that?' Julia pointed to a flash of movement. 'There. In the bushes by the wall.'

'Rats. They're doing their damnedest to eat every bulb I bury. I'm doing my damnedest to stop them, and I'm sure you can guess which of us is losing the battle.' Lexie pushed a curl out of her eye with the back of her gloved hand. 'In time, I'd like to turn the old orangery into a palm house —'

Julia grabbed her arm and pulled her to a crouch. 'That's one bloody big rat.'

'You can't possibly think it's Ezra?'

'This qualifies as familiar territory to me, and if he believes Cara was equally to blame, especially when she was such a regular visitor once the baby was born —' after the loss of two daughters on top of her son, Julia could see why '— Higgins would see her collusion as an even greater betrayal.'

'Well, that's the bugger about betrayal, Julia. It never comes from your enemies.' Lexie swallowed the sharpness out of her voice. 'Taking a pot-shot at Cara is one thing. Shooting two innocent, unarmed women is a different matter entirely.'

Naïve optimism? Or supreme confidence that the fugitive wasn't going to fire? 'People rarely think straight when they're cornered,' Julia said, thinking this definitely wasn't the behaviour of a woman worried about cat burglars on the prowl.

'What's wrong?' From the opposite side of the garden appeared a young man with gypsy good looks and muscles punching through his open-necked work shirt.

'Julia, meet Mr. Tyler, our handyman. Dickon, this is Mrs. McAllister, the photographer from Oakbourne.'

Really? Polite introductions when we're all about to swallow a mouthful of pellets?

'Mrs. McAllister thinks Ezra Higgins might be hiding in the bushes by the wall.'

Dickon looked in the direction of the wall. 'Then you two go inside. If —'

'If, if, if.' Lexie's snort echoed in the stillness. 'I can't live my life worrying about ifs and maybes, Dickon.'

'We should call the police,' Julia hissed, still crouching.

'No telephone, remember.' Was it her imagination, or did Lexie's big blue eyes flicker with anger? 'Let's rush him.'

'Let's not,' Julia said. Ezra would be ready for anything, and jittery as hell.

'Nonsense.' A garden trowel had appeared in Lexie's hand. She was holding it high, like a dagger. 'Three against one? Come along, Dickon.'

'Fine.' His expression was solemn, his body tight as a spring, his eyes black with something that wasn't fear as he picked up the rake lying on the grass. 'But Mrs. McAllister, you stay here.'

Bugger that. Julia grabbed a piece of wood from the herb bed and hefted it for balance. *The paperwork from losing my crime scene photographer doesn't bear thinking about.* Suddenly, Collingwood's joke was no longer funny.

Snaking ahead with the same stealth with which he'd appeared, the young man with olive skin and glossy black curls indicated that he'd seen, or heard, something behind a stack of broken tiles and timber in the corner. He signalled with his fingers that the three of them should spread out. Julia supposed it made sense. Higgins could only cover one direction at a time, and there were only two barrels to empty.

But down her back, sweat ran colder than the River Styx, her mouth was dry, her breath short, and her heart hammered against her ribs like a piston.

'*Hhhhhhhh.*'

She had to strain hard to hear it, but — yes. Breath. Faint. Very faint. But breath nevertheless.

What she didn't hear was the click of a shotgun. Meaning it was cocked, ready to fire.

CHAPTER 14

'Kittens?'

This wasn't quite how Julia imagined her first encounter with the gold-digger who married Henry Davenport and stepped straight into the role of stepmother. Not being covered in cobwebs and compost, with a tortoiseshell cat and two mewling kittens bundled inside her jacket, her boater midway between the cauliflowers and the azaleas, while shaking like a glass of water on the platform when the 8.10 to Waterloo came racing through. Blonde, elegant and stunningly handsome, Lydia (to make matters worse) was one of those women who undoubtedly grew up balancing books on their heads and overlapping their feet when they walked. Women who, in previous lives, were probably cats.

'Better than a desperado at the end of a barrel,' Dickon rumbled.

'They're adorable!' A young woman, eighteen at the most, rushed forward to relieve the visitor of her squirming burden, uncaring of what cat hairs and scratches might do to her Charles Worth watered-silk dress. 'I'm Grace, by the way. *Love* your outfit. Simply screams progress! So bold, so daring, with a soupçon of danger, how exciting! Can I have a bloomer suit, Mama?'

'No.' If Lydia looked thunderstruck and Grace looked elated, Lexie looked like a wasp was stuck under her tongue.

'Talk to her, Lydia. Tell her how good I'd look in one. How terribly *modern*.'

'Sorry, darling, that's between you and your mother.' Lydia smiled as she held out her hand. 'Pleasure to meet you, Mrs. McAllister, but I'm afraid you'll have to excuse me.'

'Dickon! Help me out here! Tell Mama how *practical* as well as gorgeous a bloomer suit would be. Bet they're comfortable, too. Would make climbing —'

'Grace, why don't you find a home for the cats then clean this lovely velvet jacket, while Mrs. McAllister and I take sherry on the terrace?' Lexie linked elbows with her guest. 'I think we deserve a snorter, don't you?'

'If this is a preface to your twisting my arm,' Julia said, 'trust me, I'm already sold.'

She'd only ever been inside two manor houses, but the contrast between this and Chislehurst couldn't be greater. From the instant she passed through the studded oak doorway, the difference was clear, because no matter how much the Forbes pile radiated money and power, the prevailing feature of Lindale was light. An effect maximized by cream stone complemented by soft wood tones that had no need of Canalettos and Vermeers. Mirrors bounced style and sophistication in every direction, fresh flowers added welcome, potted palms added charm, and a man could shave in the shine on the tables. If there was one thing that defined this place, Julia decided, it was love. Having said that. The smell of thinners and varnish, and yet... Not a workman in sight.

'You were quite the heroine back there,' Lexie said, pouring Oloroso into two exquisite emerald green sherry glasses.

The terrace in question overlooked the lake. There was still about an hour of daylight left, and the air was warm and perfectly still. A couple of swans, and the scene would have been complete.

'*Julia McAllister, Photographer* & *Cat Rescuer.* Think it would look good on my visiting card?'

'Perhaps you should add *Rugby Tackles A Speciality* underneath. That was quite some dive.'

When Julia tossed off her jacket and lunged at the pile of timber and tiles, she expected to be throwing it over a trigger-happy fugitive. God knows, she was no gambler, but two barrels versus three people didn't make for good odds. By catching Ezra off guard, he might shoot off one round, but there'd be no time for the second, and the chances were his aim would be skewed. All that flashed through her mind in a split-second. There was no time to weigh up options, just act. The effect on her nerves afterwards, though, left her teeth chattering like magpies, whereas whatever Lexie Davenport felt about finding a nest of cats instead of Ezra Higgins — relief, surprise, anti-climax, confusion? — she was keeping it close to her chest. The glass she held by its stem to avoid warming the intense, fragrant contents didn't waver.

'One of the side-effects of growing up with a brother,' Julia lied. 'Another was eating fast, so he won't pinch your food.'

'Sounds like a happy childhood.'

'Idyllic.' Julia lifted her face to the setting sun. If you didn't know better, you'd be forgiven for thinking nothing had changed here. The same restful vista of woodlands and fields, stretching away to infinity. The topiaried box trees, in tight, tidy pyramids. The water reflecting the cloudless blue sky. You'd think Davenport orchards still produced top quality fruit. That the arable land still belonged to the Manor. That Henry Davenport and Austin Forbes were still alive.

But that's the thing. Julia did know better. Everything had changed. Every. Single. Damned. Thing.

'What do you think of the sherry?' Lexie refilled their glasses.

'My mentor once told me that fine wines, like fine spirits, are an art form in themselves.' *Watch how it clings to the side of the glass, JJ.* Sam's voice echoed round her memory. *Let the colours play in the glass and tell me what you see. Amber? Topaz? Gold?* He'd been teaching her how to enjoy cognac, but from the moment he rescued her, he set on unleashing the artist in her. Knew that she'd seek deeper and more interesting dimensions, such as nutmeg, bulrush and rust. 'I'd say this is very fine artwork indeed.'

'A second pressing followed by forty years in the barrel gives it richness and depth.' Lexie held the glass to her nose, closed her eyes and inhaled. 'Almonds and orange peel. Hints of figs, walnuts, dates with possibly a nuance of black cherries.'

Ah, yes. Nuances. Julia sipped her liquid art. Elusive little buggers. In fact, one of her biggest challenges was capturing them so that what could easily be a run-of-the-mill photograph ended up a fully rounded portrait that reflected the sitter's character.

For instance, if Grace had been in her studio this morning, she'd have looked past the big blue eyes and caramel curls that she'd inherited from her mother, and concentrated on bringing out the girl's long, slim fingers and childlike enthusiasm. Her gaucheness, eighteen going on eight, would have been disguised through the judicious use of props.

With Lydia, she'd have accentuated her admirably tight figure and the elegance that oozed from every pore, and also played up the green eyes and lustrous blonde hair that belied a woman in her mid-forties. But how would she have hidden the sadness behind those green eyes? How would she have disguised poise that was purely for public display? Or the splatters of paint ingrained on her hands like a palette?

More importantly, if Julia was forced to photograph the three of them together, how would she prevent the picture from resembling a stage play?

As a flock of starlings flew over in a soft whirr of feathers, heading for town to roost up for the night, she was glad she didn't have to answer that question, because in many ways this crime was like the Oloroso. She held her glass up to the fading light.

Sherry was one of the oldest wines in the world, dating from the Moorish occupation of Spain when Jerez was called Sherrish, and many of the producers traced back hundreds of years. After that illustrious second pressing, the wine was fortified with grape spirit which itself had been maturing for decades in old casks, before being aged in oak and subjected to a complex process of fractional blending requiring the highest level of expertise. The sherry in Julia's glass was the oldest, the finest, forty years in the barrel. As with this house — like these grounds — and these crimes — it had been blended, tended, nurtured and loved.

A long time in the planning.

'I haven't read anything about the police re-opening the kidnap,' Lexie said.

Her nonchalance fooled no one. What she really wanted to know was, did the police think Austin's murder and his son's disappearance were linked?

'Nothing tugs at the heart strings like a missing child,' Julia said, 'but the chief superintendent is reluctant to pick the scab.' Not when he'd searched so hard, yet failed so spectacularly.

'Because he thinks the exposure will do more harm than good, by turning it into a national circus? Or because his inability to find the boy will be dragged back into the limelight?'

'You know, for someone who befriended me to get on the good side of the police, you're going a strange way about it.'

'My apologies. I'm not usually this rude.'

'You're usually this passionate, though?'

'Wouldn't you be, if you'd been a prime suspect for eight years?'

A heaviness wrapped round Julia's heart. 'Cara's already buried two babies, Lexie. She deserves the truth, even if it means another grave for the angels to pluck their strings over.'

'There are no harps where Austin's gone.'

'Medium rare with the pitchfork, you think?'

'Done to a crisp with any luck, and no better place for him. Forgive me. I don't mean to sound callous. Of course Cara needs to find out what happened to her son.' Good girl, right on cue. That elegant, trademark, butter-wouldn't-melt smile. 'On the other hand, I'm not stupid enough to think you trailed all the way out here because you lack female companionship and enjoy my wit and conversation. This is *your* crusade, isn't it? Nothing to do with the police. *You* want to find out what happened to Thomas.'

'Realistically, this is Cara's last chance.'

Twilight enveloped the terrace, bats swooped for moths over the lake, a hedgehog scuttled into the bushes. And all the while, Julia knew Lexie was mustering her thoughts. 'Everyone thinks they know me, on account of what they've read in the papers,' Lexie said finally. 'Well, I've had it to here with lies, half-truths and assumptions, and my daughter deserves better than to be tarred with suspicion. As long as we're living under this cloud, she'll never snare a good marriage.'

Was that why she dropped the brooch? To tell her side of the story? Or to feed someone with the ear of the police a well-rehearsed fiction?

'Here's what I propose.' Lexie leaned forward. 'You and I work together, Julia. Two birds with one stone. That way, Cara finds answers, I clear my name, and, as an added bonus, Grace will have suitors queuing up in the driveway.'

Lexie was sharp. She was passionate, she was perceptive, she was blunt. Julia also had a feeling that she'd revealed more of herself today than she'd revealed to another living soul in eight years. But...

Come into my parlour, said the spider to the fly.

'As ideas go —' Julia chinked glasses with an equally ingenuous smile — 'I'd say it's on a par with this sherry.'

Seriously, Lexie. Do I look like I have wings?

CHAPTER 15

Two and a half days might have passed since Ezra went on the run, but he was here at Lindale Manor, Julia was sure of it. *He'll be hungry, he'll be scared, he'll be jumpy,* Collingwood had said. But was he? Not if someone was sheltering him. Feeding him. Telling Ezra to hang tight, hold his nerve, because everything will work out in the long run.

Standing on the terrace, Julia stared up at the sky. They were between moons at the moment. The old one had died, the new not yet born. The time when midnight was blacker than obsidian, and the stars close enough to reach up and touch. Across the fields, a fox barked. A barn owl ghosted silently past.

It would have been a warm, perhaps even sultry night like this when Thomas was kidnapped. The leaves on the trees would have been ready to turn. Yellow, if the summer had been a heatwave. Red if there had been too much rain. She imagined the nurse stroking his little fat cheek as she sang maybe, who knows, the same lullaby Julia's mother sang to her night after night?

I love the White Rose in its splendour
I love the White Rose in its bloom—

She pictured the nurse smoothing his fluff of dark curls, turning the oil lamp to low, picking his stuffed rabbit off the floor where he'd dropped it, and tucking it back in beside him.

I love the White Rose so fair as she grows.
It's the rose that reminds me of you.

True, this was yet another jigsaw pieced together from gossip and newspaper articles, then glued together with imagination and logic. Julia had absolutely no way of knowing what toys

Thomas played with. Did tiny soldiers keep him amused, did he prefer trains, or was it Noah's ark with little carved animals? Did he gallop round the nursery on a hobby horse, or yeeha-cowboy on a painted rocking horse? Every child has a stuffed toy they love best, though. The thing they cuddle up to when they go to sleep, and in Thomas' case, the newspapers reported, it was a rabbit. Julia instantly named it Hoppy, and imagined the nurse regularly sewing its ears back on, re-stitching its eyes, mending its misshapen powder puff tail, and re-stuffing its stomach. She visualised the little scamp trying to take Hoppy in the bath and being told he couldn't, because Hoppy's job was to sit on the edge of the tub and report back to Papa how the nurse scrubbed the back of his neck properly, and didn't miss the bits behind his ears. Because that was the odd thing. The really odd thing. Day or night, Thomas was never alone…

Ten o'clock on the dot. The nurse's testimony didn't waiver. She'd heard the church bells in the distance, she said. Counted them out. *Time to empty your pot-pot,* she told Thomas. *I'll not be long.*

The nurse was sure — though no, she couldn't swear under oath — that she'd closed the window, and her uncertainty was understandable. The poor woman was in a terrible state. She could remember everything up to that moment "ever so clearly", she'd said. Wriggling Thomas out of his favourite little sailor suit. Tickling him in the bath. Playing him his wind-up musical carousel. Cuddling him off to sleep. She remembered smoothing her pinafore and straightening her cap. She was absolutely clear about that, since the staff were not permitted the slightest lapse in standards, and it would break her heart, she'd said, to be sacked for something as trivial as a creased uniform, or giving him milk that was too hot and made the boy cry.

Dear me, if there was even the tiniest bruise on his knee, they practically called out the police, she had added. Which is why she was sure (but couldn't swear) that she'd closed the window. Wouldn't have wanted a draught creeping in. *I was only gone a few minutes. Ten at most.*

Julia doubted the timescale, but given the servants-walking-on-eggshells environment, she calculated the size of Chislehurst Hall plus chores plus a call of nature equalled no more than twenty. Half an hour, if she'd sneaked into the kitchen for a snack. At first, the nurse didn't notice anything wrong when she returned. Assumed the stuffed rabbit had slid through the bars of the crib while her little charge slept. It was only when she went to tuck it back in that she realised the cot was empty.

Not quite empty, Julia thought, staring at the stars twinkling above. There was a ransom demand on the pillow —

Chance or premeditation? The police decided neither could be ruled out, that it could easily have been a drunken prank gone wrong, a grievance over pay, or some poisonous combination of the lot. What, other than drunkenness, explained that impossibly high ransom? A thousand pounds equated to twenty years' wages for the average agricultural worker, and whoever left the ransom note must have known that even the wealthiest businessman doesn't keep that kind of money lying around. Far safer to ask for two, even three hundred pounds. That way, the bank would not be alerted to any abnormal withdrawals, which in turn would not have alerted the police. Easy pickings in every sense.

Watching the Dragon coiling round the Little Bear overhead, Julia knew that kidnappers were driven by one of two things.

Greed. Or revenge.

If the crime was one of opportunity, it might well be that, in their haste, they bungled the job and Thomas suffocated in the process. That would explain why the ransom wasn't claimed. But suppose money wasn't the motive? In which case, the higher the demand, the greater the distraction — the theory being that as long as the spotlight stayed on the ransom, the police wouldn't look too hard elsewhere.

Except they did look hard elsewhere.

And they didn't have far to look.

Thomas was snatched seven months after Henry Davenport signed over his lands then promptly blew his brains out, leaving Lexie with a decomposing house and no money, a daughter with no chance of marrying well, as well as a stepmother she hated but couldn't get rid of. And if that wasn't enough, Forbes promptly rode roughshod over three hundred years of lovingly nurtured soil for the get-rich-quick benefits of jam production. For a woman ferociously proud of her heritage, that could easily have been the last straw.

Surely, though, only a monster would kidnap a baby to get back at a man who, legally if not morally, had done nothing wrong?

Or did the desire to get even burn so hot that it distorted perspective?

Julia remembered Lexie's calmness in the garden when faced with the possibility of trigger-happy fugitives. The steady hand on the terrace that poured the sherry. The way she'd sought out the police's scene-of-crime photographer, then laid a trail of breadcrumbs for her to follow. Contrasted with the edgy way she'd broached the connection between Austin's murder and the kidnap, and her shocked expression when Julia came up clutching nothing more menacing than a bundle of cats.

Why, too, invite a person, whose rich seam of information had run dry, to stay for dinner?

The answer, she was sure, lay in the kidnap and an amalgam of both greed and revenge. Ezra got the money. Lexie got to hurt Austin where the pain cut the deepest. Win-win. That's why Higgins wasn't a threat. Eight years ago, they were working together, motive, means and opportunity dovetailing as smoothly as the joints in Julia's mahogany camera.

Lexie was a planner. She was well placed to know the routines in Chislehurst Hall, since servants gossip like crazy, and thanks to all those society dinners and balls, she knew the layout like the back of her hand, and, since it had been in her family for generations, that the folly would make for a good ransom drop. She was in the perfect position to plan exactly how, and when, Ezra could sneak in unseen. Where he could hide. When to strike.

So what went wrong?

On the terrace, the night air thickened and twisted.

Thomas died. That's what went wrong. That's why the money wasn't collected, and that's why Ezra Higgins was knocking forty before he married and started a family of his own. The accountant, God bless him, had a conscience. It took him those six years to come to terms with what was undoubtedly an accident, but nevertheless ended in tragedy.

Jump forward to the present, and sod disgruntled tenants with eight-month-old grudges inciting mild-mannered book-keepers to murder. A woman with ingenuous blue eyes, on the other hand...

Julia heard an owl hoot in the distance, and thought it was all very well knowing who was behind the boy's kidnap and Austin Forbes' murder.

How the hell was she going to prove it?

'Oh, there you are.' Lydia's soft tones floated through the stillness. 'I thought you'd got lost.'

How else does a girl spend her time between dinner and coffee than poke around heaps of broken tiles and timber? And finding nothing more incriminating than a couple of cat hairs. 'I was enjoying these beautiful roses.' The stick Julia had picked up to defend herself made no sound when she let it fall on the grass. 'Scented night air tends to be somewhat of a rarity in Oakbourne.'

'Such a pretty town! So full of character, and the bandstand on the Common is simply charming. Catch the angle right, and you have the pond framed in a perfect circle behind it, reed beds on the left, the whole picture set off by that magnificent Lebanese Cedar.'

Julia smiled. 'You have quite the artist's eye.'

'So have you, dear. That portrait of your employer?'

'Er —?'

'In the window of your studio, on the left. I assume you took that? Who else, I suppose, but it's truly excellent, the way you played up the fall of light, capturing Mr. Whitmore to look the spitting image of Buffalo Bill, with his long hair, goatee beard and just that hint of naughty twinkle in his eyes.'

'Thank you.'

Julia did indeed take Sam's photo, and he *was* the spitting image of the famous showman who performed for the Queen's Jubilee. That was precisely why she took it out of the window after he died. It shone far too much attention on a man who was supposed to still be running the business, and that was four years ago. While the Cedar of Lebanon was struck by lightning about six months before that, becoming so dangerous that it required felling…

'Oh, look,' Lydia exclaimed. 'A shooting star!'

'Those aren't exactly ten a penny in Oakbourne, either.' In fact, if you saw stars at all, it was only thanks to the wind blowing from the west, sending the smoke over to London.

'August is the best time of year to spot them,' Lydia was saying. 'They whizz round the heavens like World Fair fireworks. Not, of course, that I've been to Chicago. Paris, on the other hand! Henry and I spent our honeymoon there, but I'm wittering. What I really wanted to say was how glad I am that you dined with us, dear. I can't tell you how good it is to have company.'

'That's the best meal I've had for ages, absolutely delicious.'

Delicious, but, like everything else where the Davenports were concerned, a mass of contradictions. A treat for the taste buds and exquisitely presented, but from the mushroom in port wine starter to the duck with cherries, right through to the blackberry tart, Julia got the impression that every ingredient had been either hunted, trapped, foraged for, or grew wild here. Yet the women's evening gowns — including this grey silk number that Lexie had loaned her — went so far beyond expensive that you'd need six hands to count the noughts.

'Duck was Henry's favourite,' Lydia said. 'Roasted with orange until the little pieces of peel turned black, then served with just the tiniest sprinkle of thyme and cayenne pepper.'

Her memory was prodigious, and it was easy to see why she'd remember her late husband's favourite dish. But what was so special about Oakbourne that left such an impression that it was preserved in her memory like a fly in amber?

And the handyman. The sultry Dickon with the olive skin, dark curls and even darker eyes, who sprang like a genie from a bottle the instant Julia pulled Lexie to the ground. Where did he fit in at Lindale Manor?

How he fitted in was easy. Very nicely thank you, was the answer. The head gardener, Joe, said he couldn't recall Dickon tackling a single project that didn't turn out well, and Julia believed it. Not a single run on the paint, not a drip on the varnish, not a nail sticking up, out of place. But one man can't refurbish a manor house on his own. Interesting, too, that Joe himself wasn't replaced when he retired, and Julia didn't believe it was coincidence that the "small army" of gardeners trickled off straight after Dickon's arrival, either. Along with most of the servants.

Grace was on oddly familiar terms with him, too. She'd sloped off after dessert, claiming it had been a long day and she was exhausted, to which Lydia's snort belied her air of refinement. 'Bed, my eye,' she said. 'That girl's off to play with the kittens.'

And unicorns dance round the maypole, Julia thought, because don't think she hadn't noticed the brown stains on Grace's elbows which her three-quarter length sleeves hadn't been able to hide. Tones identical, unless she missed her guess, to the streaks of varnish on Dickon's white shirt. Despite her childlike manner, Grace was a woman. What odds her tastes ran to stronger, more muscular mammals?

That same immaturity had inadvertently drawn attention to an over-familiarity between the handyman and her mother, when Julia was being introduced. Of course, in such a cloistered environment, informality wasn't surprising — unless there was altogether more sinister explanation for his making himself at home here? Imagine, during the course of his work, that Dickon had stumbled across Thomas' remains… Which led to blackmail…? Which in turn led to Austin Forbes' death…?

As she followed Lydia indoors, Julia was still confused why Lexie was so keen to jump a dangerous fugitive, then horrified when Julia came up with nothing more menacing than an armful of kittens. The fact that Dickon wasn't around eight years ago, didn't mean he wasn't involved somehow now. With no idea that he was being manipulated, as well...

Lindale Manor was a house of contrasts, all right.

A house full of tragedy. Of hope. Of paradise lost.

But it was also a house full of secrets.

In short, a house full of danger.

CHAPTER 16

John Collingwood sat at his desk and tried not to think about Alice. Or Julia. Or men on the run armed with shotguns. In theory, that shouldn't be difficult. The cells were rapidly filling up with vomiting drunks, foul-mouthed whores, and thieves protesting their innocence at the tops of their voices, even though no hand was ever caught redder.

'Another big fat stack of witness statements for you to wade through, sir,' the desk sergeant breezed. 'Where shall I put 'em?'

'You can swap them for that pile of reports on the chair, Tom. All signed off.'

'No peace for the wicked, sir!'

Or the men who nabbed them, it seemed. Checking that Rule 28 of the Arrest Regulations was carried out to the letter by whichever constable had been responsible for the collar was a bore, but Collingwood was damned if some slippery barrister was going to get villains off on some legal technicality on his watch. Add on categorising offences into those to put before a magistrate versus those destined for petty sessions, quarter sessions or assizes, and you'd think a detective inspector's mind wouldn't have time to deviate, much less reach for the bottle of whisky in his top drawer.

One slug. One slug couldn't do any harm.

Nor could two. Capping the bottle, he moved to the window. Somewhere up there, behind that blanket of smog, there were stars. Thousands of them, millions of them, hidden from view, constellations in perpetual movement. But it was the Big Bear, the Little Bear, Polaris and the Dragon that were the constants in the universe, and God knows, he knew all about constants. All his life, he'd known where he was headed. Any time someone asked him as a boy, *What do you want to be when you grow up?* his reply never wavered. *I'm going to be a detective inspector at Scotland Yard!* To which his father would smile fondly and tell whoever was asking *That's spelled d-o-c-t-o-r, by the way.*

The hell it was. His family were horrified — let's be blunt, ashamed — when he joined the force, but how was helping one person at a time more noble than helping hundreds, just because one was face-to-face, while the others were invariably nameless and faceless?

'You want to be a hero? Join the army,' his father had sneered.

Heroics be damned. Robert Peel's code was based on nine basic principles, with one standing head and shoulders above the rest. The prevention of crime. After seventy years, this was as relevant now as it was then, so sod his father, his family, all those friends who'd scoffed at the long hours and abysmal pay. Just like being spat on by pickpockets, sworn at by thieves, and having his shoulder dislocated when villains refused to come quietly, it was part of the job. A job that wasn't measured by the number of arrests, but by the lack of crime in Boot Street's jurisdiction.

He rubbed his eyes and pinched the bridge of his nose. How many times had he sat at his desk, Queen Victoria peering from her frame over his shoulder, congratulating himself that, at forty-one, he was the youngest DI ever to run this station? Convinced he'd make DCI before his forty-fifth birthday? In all his years of following Peel's No.1 principle, how did he end up so blinkered that he failed to prevent crime in his own bloody house? Failed to protect his own daughter.

Christ, he was so proud the day Alice won the school prize for history! How tiny she was, the first time he held her. How she'd giggle when he gave her piggy-back rides on his shoulders. What about the time she was three, and stubbed her toe?

'Which toe?' he'd asked.

'The one that ate roast beef.'

Hard to imagine one small child could bring so much joy, so much sunshine, so much love into a dark, loveless house — until the day tuberculosis followed her home. Little by little, the ulcers ate away her lungs and her energy, stealing her smile and her spirit, and there was nothing he could do. Nothing anyone could do. Or so he thought.

For Christ's sake! His fist punched the wall. It was his *job* to look for pointers! The only job he'd ever wanted had trained him to pick up on clues and notice the warning signs, and so help him, he'd missed every last one. Now, Alice was in her grave, his wife was in an asylum, and all he had left was a black, aching hole where his heart used to be, and don't let anyone tell you differently. Life is cold, and life is lonely, when failure is your only companion.

But Alice wasn't the only child the police had let down.

From the first floor window, he stared down into Boot Street, a hive of activity despite the lateness of the hour. Listened to a woman singing bawdy words to a virtuous hymn as she weaved from the Red Lion to the Rose & Crown, the baby on her hip teething on a dried pig's ear. Watched a Pekingese with a blue ribbon in its topknot yapping at a cat in the ironmonger's window, paws folded in disdain.

Was it possible? Or just wishful thinking?

That Thomas Forbes might be alive?

CHAPTER 17

Like them or not, Julia thought, Lexie's manipulative skills had to be admired. There wasn't an obstacle in her path that woman couldn't turn to her advantage, exploiting her adversary's weak points in the guise of beauty and charm. First it was her stepmother. Unless she sold up, she was saddled with her, better to have Lydia as a friend than an enemy, that way Lexie could control her, and use her to influence events. After that, it was Ezra, then Dickon . Now it was Julia's turn, except emotional manipulation is not a quick process, and in this case, she was still feeling her way. Hence the mistakes.

Since whatever secrets this house was hiding were not being given up tonight, Julia decided the best thing was to cut her losses and re-group in the morning.

'Up the stairs, turn right, third door on the left,' Lexie said, in answer to her request for directions to the water closet.

It was down to just the two of them in the drawing room now, Lydia having excused herself on the grounds that she could hardly keep her eyes open. Funny, because in Julia's experience, a stretched mouth wasn't a yawn, and besides, it was fascinating, listening to her describe Paris with forensic recall. Everywhere from Notre Dame to the Seine to the Eiffel Tower to *Les Invalides* Lydia made her feel she was there. From the peach velvet buttoned chairs to the red silk wallpaper, every detail of the hotel where she'd honeymooned was painted sharper than Constable, Canaletto and Holbein put together.

'*Two* steam-powered lifts?' What Julia would give to see that! 'Its own post office, information desk, telegraph room, even its own *bureau de change?*'

'That hotel survived the Revolution, Napoleon, the reign of two kings and it's now the toast of *La Belle Époque*, dear.' Lydia glanced at Lexie. 'Who wouldn't want to start their marriage under its magnificent domed ceilings?'

The impressionist painter, Camille Pissarro, lived there for a short while, she said. Oscar Wilde was a regular, and apparently the Prince of Wales wasn't a stranger to the place, either. With wanderlust surging through her own veins, Julia would have loved to hear more, and Lydia had shown no signs of flagging until, at a glance from Lexie, she excused herself, the coffee barely touched.

'Bed beckons,' she said, rising. 'Only youth, I'm afraid, is indefatigable.'

Lexie pushed a curl back under its pin. 'I can't argue with that.'

'Eight years ago, you'd have argued if I told you the moon circled the earth and water was wet.'

'Rubbish!' Lexie paused. 'Eight years ago, I wasn't speaking to you.'

As Lydia's laugh echoed down the hallway, Julia wondered what her reaction would be, once she realised friendship was merely one more weapon in her stepdaughter's arsenal.

Following directions to the "necessary," Julia decided that Lindale and Chislehurst did share something in common, after all. The incalculable length of the corridors! If they'd been vertical wells and you dropped a rock down, you'd never hear the splash at the end. Also, in her world, stairs were either rickety wooden things, spiral metal death traps down to newspaper basements, or, like the ones in her studio, actually had posh backs to the treads. What they were not — she ducked a branching potted palm — were sweeping seas of marble with bronze busts of various ancestors inset like shrines in the alcoves. Oh, and few stairs that she'd encountered supported gilt-edged columns, either.

Here we go. One. Two. Third on the left — good grief, what happened to poky cupboards you could barely turn round in? The water closet was large, airy, and excruciatingly modern. So new, in fact, the smell of fresh varnish was overpowering. Facing north, it probably froze your eyeballs in winter, but with summer tipping into autumn, it was refreshingly cool. The bowl was top-quality porcelain decorated with cheerful blue flowers, almost Delft in design, with a hinged cherry wood seat. Expensive, fresh, feminine and stylish. Like everything else in *Château Davenport*.

Including the women.

She pulled the chain. Washed her hands with castile soap and dried them on a primrose yellow towel embroidered with the Davenport crest. Dammit, if Collingwood wasn't allowed near the case, then Julia would go to DCI Dudley herself. Whether she could convince him that Austin's murder and his son's kidnap were connected and Lexie Davenport was the link didn't matter. The seed would be sown. Why else would Ezra Higgins steal £300, if it wasn't to pay someone off? He had a young wife, a new baby, and held a respected position. In short, he had the world at his feet, and the only way he'd rock that boat was if someone found out what happened eight years before.

Someone, for instance, like Dickon Tyler…

If Dudley didn't take Julia seriously, a gentle reminder that the press were always open to new theories meant he'd have to take it up with the chief superintendent, who in turn would have no choice but to re-open the kidnap.

'We pulled out every stop and then some to find that boy,' Blaine had told Collingwood, 'none of us slept for weeks,' and

Julia believed it. Every officer from here to John O'Groats would have been searching for Thomas. Harvest time brought a huge influx of workers, but despite an exhaustive investigation, the police couldn't find a connection, much less a grudge, between Austin and any of his itinerant labour force. Besides, every worker had stayed on until the end of the season, otherwise they wouldn't be paid. Few kidnappers have nerves of that kind of steel, either with a live toddler, or a dead one. Especially without collecting the ransom!

With outsiders ruled out, who was left?

A nursemaid in her fifties with an impeccable record? Not even the most hardened cynic would put a former nun in the frame.

Lydia radiated serenity and poise, and we all know still waters run deep. She had every reason to want revenge on Forbes, a man who drove her husband to suicide and as a result tied her to this house and forced her to be dependent on a woman who despised her. But for the kidnap of little Thomas to work, she'd need help. A random book-keeper didn't fit.

Waters didn't run still where Lexie was concerned. They boiled and churned like Alpine snow melts. From her gardens to the renovations, passion pulsed through every pore of Lindale, small wonder she'd stayed Blaine's number one suspect. She was familiar with Chislehurst, and with no sign of a struggle, no smell of chloroform (which was ridiculously hard to administer, even if you knew how), the police were convinced — and this is what damned her — that, as a mother herself, she'd know how to pick up a baby and muffle its cries. But suspicion is not proof, and without a shred of evidence, they had no cause to arrest her.

Suppose, though, Julia gave Blaine that proof?

Closing the door of the water closet, she paused at the top of the staircase, its gilded columns shooting out conspiratorial winks in the lamplight.

'By the time I left,' the head gardener said, 'she'd dismissed that many, I'd take my break not knowing whether I was seeing shadows, ghosts, or one of the few servants she'd kept on.'

Another mystery held by these walls, but one which suited Julia's purpose. Earlier, she'd seen one maid running a broom down the corridor, then the same girl ferrying bundles of sheets to the laundry, bearing out the lack of staff. And now? No one. Julia paused. By her calculations, she had three minutes before Lexie came looking. Lamps lit the corridor on the right of the stairs towards the water closet, but the left passage was dark. Darkness that had invitation written all over it.

She eased open the first door. Inside smelled musty and stale, while the second room stank worse and was every bit as bare. But as Julia's vision adjusted, things began to make sense. Lindale Manor might look a million dollars, and the gardens were stunning, but inside, the place was a wreck. Every room that wasn't used for receiving guests had been stripped and the furniture sold off, along with anything else that would raise cash, and explained the absence of servants. There was no telephone. No electricity. No gardeners. Lindale Manor was an illusion. Smoke but no mirrors, because she'd sold those off, too. Like a house of cards, one puff, and the charade would collapse —

What was that? In the blackness and silence, a girl could be forgiven fanciful thoughts, except Julia wasn't the fanciful type, and she certainly didn't believe in ghosts. This was human sobbing echoing through, but time was too tight to follow the sound. Lexie would be here any time now, and if Julia wanted proof for DCI Dudley, she wouldn't find it patting some poor servant girl on the back!

Right, then. One more room. Just one. Because, dammit, somewhere in this house lay the key to what happened to Thomas.

Ten steps in, there was a creak, then a splintering, before her foot crashed through the floorboard.

Sod's law, she couldn't get the bloody thing out.

CHAPTER 18

'You're sure Mrs. McAllister isn't here?' Collingwood's eyes scanned the vagrant in the torn shirt and ragged trousers sitting at Julia's kitchen table, systematically demolishing the contents of her pantry. Gammon, cold chicken, corned beef, meat pie, alongside radishes, tongue and pickled onions. 'She might have popped in and out without you noticing.'

'Only if she'd turned into an ant,' Billy said. 'I been rubbing that shop doorway down all bleedin' afternoon, and no one's been in and out except for me.'

The smooth woodwork bore that out, same for the window frames and sills. The glass was a bit mucky, probably a consequence of pressing against it to rub it down, but all in all, Billy Briggs was doing a fine job. 'What about the dark room? She disappears inside for hours.'

'Look, copper, I told yer. There's no bugger here but meself. Feel free to check the coal cellar, if you're worried I've done away with her and hid the body.'

'How did you know I'm a policeman?'

'The way you was scanning the room.'

He meant the way Collingwood was sizing him up. 'And Mrs. McAllister just — what? Let you help yourself to everything in the house?'

'I'm not after the family silver, if that's what you think, mate.' Billy's blue eyes twinkled in amusement. 'Place is already stripped clean.'

Collingwood's collar suddenly felt two sizes too small. He'd accepted Julia's savings, as well as the money she'd raised from selling her furniture, to fund his wife's detention in a local asylum, rather than Broadmoor. He'd already sold his house to cover the fees, but that still left a shortfall, and in the heat of the moment, he convinced himself that if the only way he could keep tabs on the woman — make certain she didn't con her way back into society — was by making a deal with the devil, then so be it. In return, he'd promised not to dig into Julia's past, but he was a policeman, for Christ's sake. And detective inspectors do not take bribes.

'This here's me payment for the windows,' Billy was saying, tapping the tabletop with his knuckles. 'As much grub as I can eat.'

Keep your friends close, but your enemies closer? Clever move.

'Coffee, copper?'

'Er —'

'Yer look like you could use something stronger, but coffee's all there is, 'cause Billy Briggs don't drink.' He poured a cup and pushed it across the table. 'Wot? Don't believe me?'

'Let's say most men that I've arrested for vagrancy wouldn't know how to spell sober if it was tattooed on their wrist.' Was it professional curiosity, an excuse for company, a need to know what she'd found out, or a desire to be close to Julia that made him take a seat?

'Yeah, well, like me dear departed daddy used to say, sincerity's everything, mate. Fake that and you'll be fine.'

Against his better judgement, Collingwood laughed. 'When did he die?'

'Not dead, just departed. Buggered off the day I turned eight, didn't even stop to wish me 'appy birthday.'

'I'm sorry.'

'Don't be. He was a drunk and a layabout, and you mightn't think it, looking at me now, but my world's a brighter place without him.'

'Is that why you're teetotal?'

'Nope.' Billy Briggs wiped his hands down the side of his trousers. 'It's the reason I keep moving, 'cause if I stop, the only place I'd go is down the neck of a bottle, and I tell yer now, it's a load of cobblers, that crap about what doesn't kill yer makes yer stronger.' He brandished a pickled onion on the end of his fork. 'Don't half make yer sick, though. Sick of waking up covered in vomit. Sick of me hands shaking too bad to cut leather for gloves. Sick of being the laughing stock of the factory. But it don't, and this is the worst bit, it don't make a man sick of living. How's that for irony, eh? Me begging on the streets, pretending I'm a soldier, when at heart I'm a soddin' great coward.'

'I'd say soldiering on, instead of giving up after whatever tipped you into that abyss, takes quite a bit of courage.'

'Red and green should never be seen.'

'Huh?'

'That's wot tipped me.' The colour drained from Billy's face. 'Green like weeping willows in the spring, that's what my Lizzie was wearing when it happened. Exact same colour of her eyes, and she'd only just bought that frock, too. What with the baby on the way, she couldn't fit into her old ones.' He scrubbed his eyes with the back of his hand and stared at the holes in his boots. 'Had to be the bloody run-up to Christmas, didn't it? Any other time, I'd have been home, suppin' ale in front the fire, feeling the baby kick. But no, no, it was the run-up to soddin', bleedin' Christmas, when everyone wants swanky gloves to put underneath the tree. So there's me, Billy clever Briggs, working extra shifts so me and Lizzie can move out of that poky room and rent a bigger place for when the nipper comes, and no idea, till I turns the corner, that the whole damn building had gone up in flames.'

Red and green should never be seen.

'I'm really sorry, Billy.'

'She weren't the only one. Six others died in that fire, but if I'd been there, I could have saved her, I bloody know I could.'

'More likely you'd have died, too.'

'And what's wrong with that?'

The heartbreak was too raw for Billy to see that his guilt was unfounded, or understand that it would fade over time, because that's what grief is. It's complex, it's dirty, and it doesn't play fair. And maybe the impulse to keep moving *was* better than trying to drink it away, but Collingwood wouldn't put money on that. 'You can't blame yourself for a rough throw of the dice.'

'Watch me.' Billy prised his eyes from the floor. Took a deep breath. Scratched his stubble. 'Look, that was two years ago. What d'yer say we put an end to this pity party and get back to the grub, before our bellies think our throats have been cut?'

A grieving widower, a grieving father, both trying to drink themselves out of their pain and both failing with spectacular success. Under normal circumstances, Collingwood wouldn't leave Briggs alone in this state, even if a choir of angels tried to prise him away.

But Julia was still out there.

Along with a killer armed with a shotgun.

CHAPTER 19

'You realise Lexie will probably bill you for the damage to her floor?'

'You mean the improvements.'

They were in the bathroom, Julia perched on the edge of the bath with her bloomer suit up and stocking rolled down, Lydia kneeling on the tiles with bloodstains all over her old-fashioned cotton tea dress, applying hot and cold compresses to an already colourful ankle.

Neither wrapper or a ball gown, but somewhere between the two, tea dresses were designed for comfort, which Lydia clearly took to mean no corset, and two things struck Julia about this. Firstly, that excusing herself for being tired was a load of rhymes-with-wobblers, or she'd be in a nightgown. But mainly because her dress was old and faded, and splurged with a palette of colourful paint spots — and since when had turpentine knocked Dior off the perfume podium?

'Let me take a look at your hand.'

'It's nothing.' Julia had already picked out the splinters. 'A scratch.'

'Scratches don't bleed like a stuck pig, dear.'

'You obviously never climbed trees as a child.'

'I firmly believed, and still do, that there are better ways to study Mr. Newton's law of gravity.' Lydia rubbed in a vile-smelling ointment based on comfrey and bay from a jar, then leaned back. 'I know this is asking an awful lot, especially when you don't even know me, but ... can I rely on you to keep our secret?'

'There's no shame in poverty, Lydia.'

'As opposed to the shame in snooping round other people's houses?'

Julia winced, and it had nothing to do with the stench. 'Ten minutes ago, I justified it by telling myself that I work with the police and owe it to Cara Forbes. Right now, I don't feel so lofty.'

'Humiliation hurts, doesn't it?' Lydia returned to the ankle, applying a poultice of parsley and comfrey to reduce the swelling. 'Multiply that by a thousand and that's what we're — what Lexie — is facing, should our circumstances become public knowledge.'

'Why is keeping up appearances so important?'

There was a long pause. A very long pause. Julia thought back to when she was fighting to free her foot and a vision of blonde loveliness appeared in the doorway. In the dark, she hadn't been able to tell if that was a smile or a scowl on the older woman's face. Neither would have made her feel better.

'After Henry died,' Lydia said at last, 'I had nothing. No money. No prospects. Just a roof over my head for as long as I lived, a roof I was forced to share with a woman who made no bones about her feelings towards me, and if she sold up, as Broadhurst expected, I wouldn't even have had that. Instead, she called me in to her room, sat me down, told me that I was a Davenport now and Davenports don't back away from a fight. That they face trouble head on, and win.'

Was Lydia crying? The memories of her honeymoon suddenly overwhelming her? Or the loneliness of her husband's passing…?

Lydia tipped the bloodied water out of the china basin. 'Running the estate gave her what I believe you modern girls call tunnel vision. It was only after her father passed that she realised the depth of the neglect, but reasoned, how hard could it be to restore Lindale to its original glory?' She screwed the lid back on the jar. 'The woodworm answered that question straight off, and the further the builders probed, the more dry rot they found, the deeper the damp, and why we hadn't all died from lead in the pipes was beyond them.'

At first, she said, Lexie accused them of exaggerating to bump up the bill. But after being half-drowned from a burst pipe, almost brained by yet another loose tile off the roof, and then doing exactly what Julia did, going straight through the floorboards, the message finally sank in.

'How does a single lady fund renovations without collateral?' Lydia snorted. 'Lexie was laughed out of every bank from here to infinity, and that, dear, is why keeping up appearances is so important.'

To paraphrase the delivery man tossing sacks to the grocer, *free access to the gardens, my arse*. Julia knew now that the botanical "rooms" were nothing but an advertisement for Davenport wealth, and in order to maintain the pretence, Lexie needed to impress people beyond just these walls. Hence the expensive powder blue outfit this morning, the rare feathers in her hat, and wearing every last jewel she had left when she dropped by the studio. And if, by some miracle, there were any members of Oakbourne society who'd missed her sweeping through like a ship in full sail, she'd lay odds that the charade with the motorized Benz put that right. Did Lexie pay the tricycle driver, or merely time it to a fault? *She's a right perfectionist, that one*. Either way, that outfit cost too much to let tyre treads spoil it.

Sam used to joke that a secret was something you only tell one person at a time, but this went beyond keeping confidences.

This was about Thomas.

It was only when Julia's foot was stuck solid, and no amount of scratching or pulling or kicking could free it, topped by the very real possibility that the whole floor could collapse, that she understood the true meaning of helplessness. In her case, Lydia was able to lever her loose and she was only trapped for a few minutes. But Thomas?

Eight years ago, a child was abducted and his parents couldn't call the police, tell anyone, or ask for help. They could only wait. Two agonising days later, when the ransom wasn't touched and they finally contacted the then-DCI Blaine, they found themselves locked in a vacuum of powerlessness and dread, from which there was no escape. Austin and Cara, though, were adults. Alone, terrified, surrounded by unfamiliar sounds and foreign smells, Thomas didn't have the luxury of understanding. Did he cry? Scream? Call for his mama? Did a hand, a cloth, (a bosom smelling of sandalwood, vanilla and patchouli?) stifle his blubbing? With truly disastrous results —?

'When a small, helpless creature has no voice of his own,' Julia said quietly, 'someone needs to speak for him.'

Lydia swallowed. Reached for another jar, this time one with an infinitely more agreeable perfume. 'Calendula,' she said. 'Marigolds, if your Latin's not quite up to scratch. Good for ulcers and open wounds, too. Very soothing.' She pretended to concentrate on wrapping a bandage round Julia's ankle. 'On a … scale of one to ten,' she said at last, 'where do you rate your chances of finding what happened to him?'

Had she noticed that Julia hadn't agreed to keep the Davenport's dire financial situation to herself? 'Eight. Nine.'

'*Really?*' There was no disguising the surprise on Lydia's face, or the suggestion in her voice that she'd have rated it two. At the most.

'Just because a scent has gone stale, it doesn't mean it's not there.'

Lexie was behind this. Every stone, every tile, every marble stair in Lindale said so, it was only a question of proof.

Lydia pinned the bandage in place. 'Can you stand?'

'I'm fit to run a marath—' Julia grabbed the edge of the bath.

'Darling, you couldn't run up a bill.' Lydia smoothed her paint-splattered, blood-splattered dress as though it was fresh from the dressmaker's dummy. 'I rather think you're with us for the night.'

'Are you *mad*?' Through the crack in the morning room door, Julia watched Lexie's eyes bulge in horror. 'For God's sake, what were you thinking, letting her sleep here?'

'What was I supposed to do?' Lydia set down a tray with teapot and two cups on the side table. 'The girl can't walk, much less cycle all the way to Oakbourne.'

'There are such things as hansom cabs.'

'We don't have a telephone.'

'We have horses.'

'Without Dickon, will it be you or me saddling the brute then riding to town to summon a cab?'

'Fair point.'

The morning room was as far removed from the drawing room as you could imagine. Even through the crack, Julia could see that the vibrant blue wallpaper had faded to grey, except for sad rectangles where pictures used to hang. The parquet was pitted and splintered.

'You engineered this visit by dropping your brooch, and she saw straight through it, dear. Now, she's already said the police have linked Austin's murder to the abduction, and it's obvious that she's not going to rest until she finds out what happened to Thomas. Where's the harm in trying a different tack, and show her we have nothing to hide?'

'If that's a joke, it's in very poor taste. What if she sees —'

'I've already slipped something in her milk, she'll sleep like a baby.'

'Then I suggest we turn this to our advantage.'

'I fail to see how. I'll call Grace and Dickon —'

'Nonsense. This is the perfect, perhaps the only, way for us to have the spotlight lifted, and remember, Lydia. I still hold all the aces.'

'Lately, dear, it feels more like aces and eights.' Dead man's hand. 'But you're right. We've played with fire before, and ridden worse storms in the past. All we have to do is keep calm —'

'— keep smiling —'

'— keep pretending like always. Between us, we're more than a match for some upstart who's convinced she can find a missing boy after eight years, when the resources of an entire police force were unable to.'

'Don't underestimate this woman, Lydia. The biggest mistake we can make right now is losing Julia McAllister's trust.'

'I know, I'm sorry. I didn't mean to snap.' Lydia sank into one of the faded velvet chairs with characteristic grace. 'I'm just edgy.'

'Don't apologise. We both are.' Lexie spiked her hands through her curls. 'It's odd, really. I imagined I'd be relieved, at the very least, now that Austin is dead.'

'But?'

'I just feel incredibly, bone-weary sad. In fact, more annoyed than anything, how ridiculous is that?'

'It's because you don't have anyone to hate any more. A lost sense of purpose, if you like.'

'Seriously, Lydia? When I have damp, dry rot and woodworm jostling for first place on the honours list and a daughter in dire need of a dowry, yet here I am, splashing a fortune on finery to impress society, while Dickon's trapping food and you're brewing herbal infusions, because we can't afford tea.'

'Are you saying you don't like my spicy blend of chamomile, cinnamon and apple?'

'Of course not. It's delicious.' Lexie held up her cup. 'But look at us! Drinking from porcelain so fine you can read the tax demands through it.'

'So tonight ... what? We have what is effectively a police spy under our roof and you advocate business as usual?'

'Warfare is based on deception and planning.' With great care, Lexie replaced her cup in the saucer. 'Have faith, Lydia. This is a war I *will* win.'

At what cost, though? Julia wondered, before slipping quietly back to her bedroom.

Fireflies danced in the bushes. A nightingale sang its sweet, fluid song in the woods. Julia's ankle throbbed like blue bloody murder.

Standing at the bedroom window, staring into the blackness, she tried to look at the land through Davenport eyes. Land that had been nurtured and farmed for three hundred years, but nothing, even the land, stays the same. Where these fields once grew wheat, the opening up of the American prairies combined with innovative reaper-binding machines plus cheap transportation, thanks to railways and steamships, effectively put British wheat out of business. With true landed gentry flair, the Davenports turned to farming a wide range of produce, with the emphasis on freshness and quality, but already the age of the millionaire landowner was being eclipsed by the age of the millionaire industrialist.

Jam production was hard, heavy work, but the end result served thousands, rather than hundreds. Consequently, Austin would consider the ripping up of old practices as natural progression. Lexie would see it as rape of the land.

Never did anything by halves, him.

The same could be said of her, though. Imagine the pain that ripped through her heart as the ploughshare churned up field upon field of seasonal produce. Carrots, celery, lettuce and peas, cabbages, beetroots and onions. Oh, how the knife would have twisted as her precious soil was re-planted with berries destined for the indignity of being squashed, boiled and potted.

Already resentful, and probably jealous that her father brought a new wife home as a *fait accompli*, a youthful beauty at that, did she once stop to question that they might have actually married for love? No, she blithely branded the usurper a gold-digger and refused to set foot in the main house, focusing instead on running the farm with rabid efficiency to the extent that she was oblivious to Henry's abdication of responsibility when it came to renovation. And after he died, she wasted no time — a mere three weeks after his funeral, Joe had said — in reversing the situation with any means at her disposal, starting with the botanical gardens.

Lydia called it tunnel vision.

Julia called it stubborn, selfish, and many other less flattering things, but that was beside the point. For eight years, Lexie had been pulling the strings of revenge. Now was the time for Julia to cut them, before anyone else got hurt.

Including her.

'Where are you, Thomas?' she whispered into the night.

But the night, like everything else around here, hung on to its secrets.

Including why Henry Davenport, with centuries of landed gentry blood running through his veins, let the place slide into such disrepair. Woodworm and damp don't move in overnight. This was years in the making. Was he a miser? Lazy? Blinkered? Blind? An ostrich who buried his head in the sand and pretended not to notice? Lydia would have noticed. She had total recall of every last detail. Why didn't she say something? Do something? Work towards putting it right?

Julia plumped down on the bed and massaged her ankle.

So many questions. No answers.

When Austin vacated the marital bed on his wife's twenty-fifth birthday, Cara didn't just lose her husband. She lost all chance of bearing another child. What prompted that departure? Julia's experience with photography told her that, more often than not, dashing middle-aged husbands had frumpy, middle-aged wives, whose doughy faces, double chins and monobosoms testified to years of letting themselves go. Small wonder so many took mistresses. Cara, though, was neither dowdy or fat, and if she was handsome on the cusp of fifty, she must have been stunning when she married Austin. Many women fall into a deep melancholy after childbirth. Had he mistaken depression for frigidity? Was that why he slept with every woman he could lay his well-manicured hands on?

The reconciliation was no less puzzling. Whatever instigated it — and however fleeting — Julia could only imagine Cara's excitement at finding herself pregnant. Here she was, forty years old and, against all the odds, with a baby that survived more than a week. How close the two of them would have grown! She pictured mother and son rolling around on the lawn. Cara tickling his fat little tummy. Biting a nervous knuckle when he took his first steps. Giggling when she tossed a ball he never caught.

Then, in the blink of an eye, he was gone.

Browbeaten, anguished, grieving and heartbroken, she'd been brought to her knees, but, just like her husband, continued to pretend to the world that her life was perfect.

Surely Lexie — a mother herself — couldn't be so blinded by hate that she failed to consider the hurt she'd cause Cara? And once she'd taken the boy, what did she do? Give him to the gypsies? In the darkness, Julia rolled her eyes. The only way that could sound more far-fetched was if she'd said she'd sold him! Adoption, then. Few couples desperate for children ask questions, and when you consider how virtually every society lady was involved in charitable works of one sort or another, it was reasonable to assume Lexie would have plenty of contacts.

Except…

Christian charity were never Mr. Austin's strong point.

Nor was it Lexie's. Hands-on with a vengeance when it came to estate management, what odds that hard work and single-minded determination left her merely hovering at the fringe of any local trusts and organizations? Attending only those events which she'd been obliged to? A situation that wouldn't have changed, once she began pasting a crumbling Lindale back together.

Julia lay back on the pillows and folded her hands behind her head.

In contrast, Lydia had never lifted a finger in her life. She was young, attractive, charming, the original trophy wife. How did a woman like that pass her time, if not with charitable causes? A woman who had equal reason to hate Austin, the man who'd taken everything from her?

Equal reason... Equality... Suddenly Julia understood the lack of servants, gardeners and tradesmen. The tacky varnish on the banister rails. The stains on Grace's elbows, the paint splashes on Lydia's hands and dress, the reason Lexie wore gloves. She wore them to hide work-worn hands. *Morning till night, you'd see her planting, pruning, pulling up pondweed,* Joe had said of Lexie. A woman driven by pride, status, and independence — qualities she'd used to sway her stepmother and daughter to the point where, with the help of Dickon Tyler, it was just the three of them working to renovate the house.

As the fireflies danced and the nightingale sang, a picture began to form at the back of Julia's mind.

And she didn't like what she was seeing.

CHAPTER 20

'What's this? National Waif and Stray Week?' Julia asked.

Lexie's ingenuous smile was fixed firmly in place. 'Breakfast in bed is all part of the package.' She hadn't yet pinned up her hair this morning. Caramel curls tumbled over her shoulders.

'I didn't realise Lindale was a hotel.'

'Only for the walking wounded.' Lexie set the tray beside the bed, then opened the curtains and window. 'In case you hadn't noticed, we're a little short on luxury upstairs.'

Not here. Not with its chocolate and gold drapes, crystal chandeliers and fine cream upholstery. 'Long on woodworm, though.'

'They're our best guests.' Lexie poured coffee from a silver pot engraved with swags and bows. Outside, the sun rose over the treetops, and the breeze was refreshing and warm. 'I forget, how do you like your coffee?'

'Same way I like my men,' Julia said. 'Strong. How do you take yours?'

'Weak, like most people I've encountered.' Lexie handed Julia the cup. 'Present company excepted.'

'I'll bet you say that to every guest you wake up in the morning.'

This time the smile was genuine. 'Only those on crutches. How's the ankle?'

'Could be worse.'

'Could be better, I dare say, and I'm sorry you had to discover our secret in such a painful way. You … slept well?'

'Lydia brought me a glass of warm milk, but between you and me, I think she doctored it. I went out like a light.'

'She's very good with herbs.' Lexie picked up the empty glass from the nightstand and put it on the tray, little knowing the contents had been tipped down the lavatory. 'Besides. Sleep is a great healer.'

Very good with herbs, eh? 'Thank you for the nightgown, and I'm grateful to you for giving up your bedroom.'

'Not a hardship, I'm afraid.' Lexie's face twisted. 'This was my grandmother's room, and I still can't rid myself of the notion that she's going to walk in any second, reciting the Bible as was her wont, and reclaim the bed in which she'd died clutching her crucifix.' The toast froze on the way to Julia's mouth. 'After my father so considerately blew his brains out all over the study, Grace and I moved back to the main house, and, given the state of the rooms, there wasn't much choice. Even so, this room has never felt comfortable. Never quite home, if you know what I mean.'

That might go some way to explaining why there were no personal possessions on show. But only some way... Julia put the toast back on the plate. 'You found your father?'

'Lydia. I was living and working out of the West Wing, but she heard the shot, went running... They needed an axe to break through in the end, and I'm afraid she took it badly.' Lexie sank down on the edge of the bed. 'All that blood. Bone. Other ... stuff ... on the walls, the desk, the ceiling. Still dripping.' She shuddered. 'There was nothing left of — of Papa's head —'

Julia resisted the urge to reach out and hug her. 'I'm so sorry. For both of you.' Unlike her adversary, she must not overplay this.

'I'm not sure Lydia will ever get over it.' Lexie balled her hands into fists. Stared at a point on the horizon. 'Strange, really. When someone's confronted with tragedy, you'd imagine they'd rush forward to comfort the person they've lost, even though the situation is hopeless. Me, I was horrified by the mess, revolted by the stench, and the price I paid for my lack of compassion was having to live with that shame. Day after day, Julia. Year after year. Knowing my only thought, when I ran through the door, was for myself, not my father.' She shook her lovely caramel curls. 'You can't begin to imagine the guilt.'

'Oh, I can. Believe me, I can.' Julia would never forgive herself for running off and hiding, disgusted by the sight of her father's corpse after he'd slipped, bone-weary, poor sod, at the end of his shift, hundreds of feet down the mineshaft. 'What you need to remember is that this is human reaction at its most basic. Ugly or not, Lexie, it's unedifyingly normal. We can't blame ourselves for instinctive reaction.'

It's only later, once the shock has passed and senses have come to terms with what happened, that objective emotions take over. In Julia's case, perhaps because she was only six at the time, it just happened to take several years.

'I couldn't then, and I still can't, believe my own father was capable of such a terrible act.'

'Suicide is the ultimate act of despair —'

'Not taking his life! I don't know what made him do it, though I wish to God I did, because I'd like to think I could have prevented it. But … to blow his head off? Knowing that's how we'd find him?'

'People in those situations don't think straight.'

'Really? Because I'm pretty sure he was thinking straight when he signed away our land and squandered mine and his granddaughter's birthright. And he was certainly thinking straight when he locked — locked! — the door to the office.

The sheer selfishness of it beggars belief, and I can't forgive him for that, Julia. Ever.'

'Him? Or yourself?' Julia blew on her coffee to cool it. 'Is that why you didn't re-marry?'

'Oh, please.' Lexie jumped off the bed. 'Do you really think I'm so shallow as to worry some man would — what? Abandon me like my father? Turn out to be as cowardly as him? Trek halfway round the world to die like my husband? After I was widowed, men were buzzing round like flies on dead meat, but not on account of my beauty, my charm, my personality, my brains. Oh, no. I represented nothing more than a business merger, the prize who'd inherit the estate. Well, guess what? When Henry Davenport died and word got round that we were penniless, the flies buzzed off, and I can honestly say I've never looked back.'

She walked over to the window.

'I must ask Dickon to build a little arched bridge for the Japanese garden. If he paints it red, people will take a lot of pleasure crossing it. Oh, I need to make sure the maples are well protected through the winter months, too.' She smiled. 'Wouldn't it be lovely if we can open the gardens for the spring blossoms, after all?'

By spring, her neck will have been stretched on the gallows, but in order for that to happen, Julia still needed that proof. She'd pretended her ankle couldn't support her weight to wangle more time in the house, a ruse that paid dividends when she'd put her ear to the door last night, because now she was in a position to add conspiracy and collusion to the list she gave DCI Dudley. *Very good with herbs* would explain why Thomas didn't cry out — while suggesting an alternative theory to shock having left the nurse's memory fuzzy.

A long time in the planning…

'You don't really blame your husband for dying in Africa?'

'Edmund. His name was Edmund.' Lexie fished out a gold locket from around her neck. Inside was a picture of a young man, resplendent in his army uniform. Ever young. Ever handsome. 'And no. I blame myself for marrying him.'

'If he'd married another girl, the timings would have been different, and he wouldn't have been killed in Amoaful?'

'I know how it sounds, Julia, and before you say anything, yes, he'd probably have been killed in a different battle, or died of disease.'

'The difference being, you wouldn't have known about it.'

'I think what hurts most is that my father was right. *A soldier? Are you mad?* he said when I told him. Naturally, I reminded him how Edmund was landed gentry same as us, that he knew how the system worked, and once he'd slain his dragons, as young men must do, he'd be an asset to Lindale. *You just wait, Papa,* I said.'

'He still didn't approve?'

'I'll be frank, Julia, there wasn't much my father did approve of. His reply, and I quote, was *He's a soldier. Feckless, drunkards and gamblers, the lot of them. Mark my words, Alexandra, that man will let you down like a pair of cheap stockings.*' Sometimes at night, she said, with the Milky Way spread across the sky and the air alive with crickets, she'd look up at the moon and hear the orchestra playing Strauss in the ballroom. She would feel the wool of his uniform under her fingers. The room swirling, as they waltzed round and round. 'Handsome, dashing, fearless Edmund,' she said, snapping the locket shut. 'Who went on to prove my father right.'

Maybe not a pair of cheap stockings, but he let her down all right. By dying on the other side of the world, unaware that his bride was with child.

As Lexie left with the breakfast tray, Julia knew that every father wants their daughter to marry well, but Henry Davenport's low opinion of her choice wasn't simply unjustified, it was an attack on the army. A line from Hamlet sprang to mind. *The lady doth protest too much.* Or in this case, the father. The same father who went home and killed himself. Out of shame? Julia eased her bandaged foot into her pumps. Or an urgent need to cover something up before word got out? Her involvement in the French postcard trade proved there were outlets for every perversion, as well as clubs catering for every conceivable vice, in which more debts were run up than any bank. Was that the reason behind Henry's so-called gift? His land in exchange for Austin settling his debts? It explained why the police found no hint of financial trouble. Unless it was blatant — imminent bankruptcy, for example — they have more pressing calls on their time than investigating legitimate contracts, however bizarre they might be.

There's no shame in poverty, Julia told Lydia last night. That was true. But there's shame in how you acquire it.

It was purely by chance, taking a last lingering look at the ornamental lake (where better than to weight a small body?) that she noticed the shadow under her window. Watched a young man with olive skin and dark, gypsy curls prise himself away from the wall. And pad back to whatever handyman skills he was supposed to be engaged in.

CHAPTER 21

'I can't thank you enough for dropping everything to come over.'

'As I said on the telephone, Cara, it's no trouble at all.'

Mrs. Forbes was waiting for Julia in the shade of the portico at Chislehurst Hall, swathes of black lace at her cuffs and her throat, frills of black silk forming a train, and Julia wasn't fooled by the high-boned collar. She'd seen it a million times in her studio, acting like a neck brace, because whether one liked it or not, keeping one's head high was important. At no time must appearances or standards be allowed to slip, and if anyone was a dab hand at masking their feelings, that person was Cara.

'When you said you were sending a driver, though, I was expecting the brougham, not a motorcar.'

Billy nearly fell off the ladder when it pulled up. 'You're not getting in that thing?'

'Think of it as another lump of machinery, Billy.' A smart, pioneering, expensive lump of machinery. Damn right she was getting in that thing!

'No roof, just four spokey wheels and a stinky petrol engine? What's to keep that car on the road?'

'Less is more, and this is a lessless age, haven't you heard? Loveless couple get legless, marry in recklessness, drive off in horseless carriage, receive congratulations by wireless telegraph, end up homeless, and it's all perfectly seamless?'

'That contraption's reckless, right enough. In fact, if I was the religious type, I'd say a prayer for yer. Instead, I just 'ope you've made a will.'

More restrained than the steam-powered quadricycle it superseded, the roadster's Cretan blue coachworks and revolutionary lines turned heads at every turn as it passed through Oakbourne. Only one old man raised his fist. Only six women screamed. Only four horses and two small dogs bolted. For the chauffeur, negotiating gears and gradients in leather cap and goggles, this represented heart-warming progress. Once clear of the town (for which read pedestrians), he opened the car up, hitting speeds of twelve miles an hour on the straight.

Back in June, forty-six such "contraptions" raced from Paris to Bordeaux and back. Two Peugeots, interestingly the same model as this, made the fastest times, but since the race was officially for four-seaters, the two two-seaters didn't count. The rally was enough to fire the public's imagination, though. There were plans to hold one every year now, and oh, what Julia wouldn't give to take part! What photographs, too. Capturing the cars as they whizzed past!

'I've penned a letter to your employer, thanking him for giving you time off,' Cara was saying. 'He must be terribly understanding, sparing you at such short notice. I'll reimburse you for whatever he docks from your pay, and then double it. Thanks to you, the knots in my stomach are beginning to unwind, I couldn't sleep a wink. In the cold light of day it seems ridiculous, mistaking shadows for stalking figures, thinking the reflection of moonlight on glass is the flash of a knife, confusing a simple draught for breath on my neck.'

'Shhh. Can you hear that?'

'The wind in the branches?'

'The sound of your demons, scuttling back to hell.'

'The Gibson Girl to the rescue, as always!' Cara clutched Julia's hand in both of hers. 'To be honest, I worried you'd grown weary of rushing to the aid of damsels in distress.'

'Still no news of Ezra?' Julia asked, as they retreated inside.

'No, but … today, I feel sure, will be a good day. A better day. Today, they will find him and finally this … this *nightmare* will be over.' She turned, her voice breaking. 'I can't take it much longer.'

Should Julia tell her the theory about Ezra and Lexie working together in the kidnap? That Dickon Tyler had somehow found out and could have been blackmailing Ezra, which triggered this latest phase in the nightmare? Absolutely, categorically not!

'Feel free to say no,' Cara was saying. 'It's a massive imposition, but the reason I asked you over … would you mind helping me sort through Austin's effects?' She tugged at her earlobe, probably the nearest she came to losing control in public. 'I can't trust anyone else. Did you see that piece in last night's *Gazette*?'

Julia nodded. *WIDOW TERRIFIED!* the headline read, going on to say how Mrs. Forbes had become a prisoner in her own home, cowering on the floor in case Higgins took a pot-shot, before detailing the shocking effects nervous exhaustion had taken on her health.

'It's bad enough having the press splashing lies across the front page — again! But to find out that a trusted servant, my own footman, peddled this slander defies belief.'

That's the bugger about betrayal, Julia. Lexie's voice drifted back. *It never comes from your enemies.*

At the end of another long and soulless corridor, which no amount of fine art could cheer up, Cara stopped and wiped her hands down the side of her dress. 'This is silly,' she said. 'It's been years since I was last in this room, I don't know why I'm nervous. Austin's hardly going to jump out at me, is he?' She turned the knob. No one jumped out. 'You see? I told you it was silly.'

As she switched on the light, Julia took in the panelled walls, ornate chandelier and Rococo bed, complete with rounded headboard in the shape of a crown. King Austin? Like the rest of Chislehurst, the room was besieged with antiques. So expensive, so tasteful, so claustrophobically repugnant. Especially the heavy gilt glass display case, although to be fair, the ribbon scroll work was exquisite.

Cara cleared her throat. 'Right then.' She reached for the sheet of paper in her pocket, on which was a short, typewritten list. 'With lists, there is order,' she said dully. 'With order, there is discipline. With discipline, there is control.'

Until you've lived it, you can't understand. Julia's mother used to line up the cups like soldiers on parade, every one in perfect alignment...

'Number one on the list. Clothes.'

'What exactly am I looking for, Cara?'

'Letters, notes, anything of a personal nature —'

'You mean compromising?'

Cara tilted her chin. 'After that perfidious footman, I daren't risk private correspondence falling into the wrong hands.' The smell of mothballs when she opened the wardrobe made both their eyes water. Covering her nose with her sleeve, Cara began checking her husband's pockets, while Julia rifled through drawers of collars, cravats, silk combinations and suspenders. Who'd have thought one man could need so many clothes?

'Nothing?'

'Nothing.'

What a relief when Cara closed the door on the mothballs!

'Number two — *oh!*'

Julia spun round, to find Cara staring at a full-length mirror, a look of shock on her face. 'What's the matter? What's wrong?'

'I — I suddenly remembered my wedding day.'

'Do you want to talk about it?'

The ceremony had taken place barely an hour before, Cara whispered. She'd come up to powder her nose. Downstairs, the crowds had spilled on to the lawns, chinking glasses and laughing in the summer sunshine. Violins were playing Vivaldi's *Four Seasons*. *Spring*, remembered it clearly, and champagne corks were popping like artillery fire as the new bride twirled the wedding band round her finger. Staring at the big Rococo bed, the house so new the room still smelled of paint, she hadn't been aware of the bedroom door opening. Only the click of the lock as Austin closed it behind him.

'What was it you saw in the mirror, Cara? What was in the reflection?'

'Triumph.' She grabbed a shirt from the drawer and threw it over the mirror. The colour returned to her cheeks. 'Right then! I'll take the shoe cabinets, scarf drawers and hat boxes, if you wouldn't mind going through the dresser.'

As you'd expect from a man who led an orderly life, there were no letters, compromising or otherwise, in his personal effects, although, to be honest, Julia was surprised at the amount of clutter Austin had accumulated, finding it hard to distinguish valuable pieces from — well, let's be honest, junk. There was also something repugnant about fishing through his leather vanity case containing clothes brushes, combs and pomades, as well as his set of silver hairbrushes. But if there were letters squirrelled away, they weren't in the box of dominoes (although she was curious as to who he played with), and the biscuit barrel contained nothing but shortbreads so stale they could serve as clay pigeons.

'Still nothing?'

'Still nothing.'

With a heavy sigh, Cara reached under his pillow and jumped. No more than four inches by six, her discovery was padded and bound with finely tooled leather, the front inset with gold and mother-of-pearl.

'What is it? A diary?'

'Must be!' Cara lifted the clasp, opened it, then dropped it with a scream that made the chandelier rattle. As she ran from the room, hands over her mouth, Julia could see that it was a photograph frame, and Cara's reaction became clear. This was a picture she hadn't seen for over eight years. Of a small face, surrounded by a fluff of dark curls, smiling above his favourite white and blue sailor suit.

Thomas's very last photo.

First-hand, Julia knew how losing someone you should have protected, and whose life you'd have instantly swapped for your own, left a pain so deep and so raw that you need to obliterate it. Destroy any trace that it ever existed. In her case, by walking away from her mother and brother, knowing she'd never see them again, there had been nothing to destroy. Merely abandon. Now it was obvious why there were no portraits of Thomas lining the corridors. No photographs of him in the drawing room. Even tough, ruthless, uncompromising Austin kept only the one photo. A picture so painful to look at, and yet so precious, that he'd kept it under his pillow.

What else did he keep hidden away?

Tempted as she was to rush after Cara, Julia knew better than to offer comfort to a woman who'd spent years suppressing her emotions. The drawbridge would come up, and instead of helping, all Julia would be doing was making it worse by not giving her the outlet she needed. If she wanted to help, then the best way to go about it was finish the search. As she turned to prop the picture on the mantelpiece, her elbow knocked a pair of opera glasses off the dressing table. Sod that. Her ankle was too sore to take her bent weight. She stepped over them, then stopped. Why would such a meticulous individual keep opera glasses handy, out of their case? She drew the curtains, picked the glasses off the floor with a wince, and directed them at the point where Austin would have stood in order to lay them back on the dresser.

The focus landed straight on the folly.

She replaced them, closed the curtains, caught the eye of a bewigged countess painted by Joshua Reynolds, as far from the vibrancy of modern Impressionism as it was possible to get. This is where Lydia's skills would come into their own, she thought. In an ideal world, crime scene photographers would also be victim photographers / suspect photographers / suspicious items photographers, cataloguing every aspect of every case. Instead, she'd just have to memorise as much as she could, adopting Lydia's talent for visual recall that she'd be able to remember every damn knick-knack in the display case, from the tortoiseshell snuff box to the gold and ivory toothpick case inset with a lock of faded red hair that was obviously not Cara's. (Austin's mother's?)

Hello, hello, hello, what was this doing among such fine antiques? Even Julia's untrained eye knew the shepherdess figurine was cheap porcelain, while the silver cufflinks engraved with a stag were already starting to tarnish. Senses suddenly on high alert, she realised the anomalies didn't stop there. That clothes brush was closer to badger bristles than boar — and what about this hideous olivewood pipe carved like a bottle, and the cheap bamboo shooting stick? She undid the stopper of his cologne bottle. Bergamot and limes, an expensive and probably personalised blend. Why would a man with more money than he can spend in a lifetime splash out on costly cologne, yet hoard a ton of cheap knick-knacks? Still. Whether they were reminders of his working class roots, or Austin was simply a hoarder (many self-made millionaires are), as a hard-nosed businessman, he'd still know how to protect his secrets. Empty pockets were in keeping with a man who was obsessively tidy and careful, but while he had a fleet of clerks tending to his business affairs, he was also someone who'd keep his personal matters very private indeed.

The Dutch cylinder writing desk, inlaid with floral marquetry patterns, was filled with predictably fine linen stationery and exquisite writing materials, and, unfortunately, correspondence bland enough to make the woodworm throw up. Even so... You can't hide secrets from an expert. Half a minute later, Julia hit pay dirt. And she didn't just hit it once, she hit it twice over.

Her first find was a wallet, taped to the underside of the drawer, containing two pieces of paper.

Her second was a stash of letters tucked in a secret compartment. Each marked *Return to Sender*. Julia opened them.

9th September, 1887.

My darling Lydia,

Twenty-eight weeks have passed since that tryst at the folly. Twenty-eight weeks to the day, during which you have returned each of my letters unopened, refused countless telegrams, and will not allow me to set foot through your door.

In short, twenty-eight weeks since you said you never wanted to see me again, but I beg you, yes beg you, to hear me out. This explanation doesn't come easily, darling, and I don't know even where to begin. Except, perhaps, with my fear.

Fear that I will never see you again. Never hold you in my arms. Never kiss you.

Fear that you believed I was laying claim to you that sunny winter's afternoon. Taking you crudely, as though you were the last piece in my conquest of Lindale Manor. Nothing could be further from the truth, but, dearest, how can I begin to put my thoughts into words? Barely one hour before I met with you, I'd walked out of the solicitor's office with your husband's land assigned to my name. No wonder you hate me.

I vowed to tell no one of my reasons, not even you. I promised Henry that I would go to my grave protecting the reputation of one of the finest families in Broadhurst, and that whatever accusations were levelled against me were irrelevant. My shoulders are broad.

I was a fool. Worse, Lydia, an arrogant fool. You'd told me how your husband had frittered away his name and his heritage, and I knew the day would come when the debts were called in. I could not, would not, stand by and let him humiliate you by having the bailiffs move in!

Then I saw you waiting for me at the folly. We are not Romeo and Juliet, you and I. We are two mature people, who'd believed our lives were set on a rigid course with all chances of happiness behind us, taking whatever pleasure we could in each passing day. How could we have been so blind?

Our lives are not over. They are in front of us, Lydia. I knew it the second I saw the sun shining on the first silver threads in your beautiful blonde hair, and the laughter lines round your mouth.

Love is not the preserve of the young. Love is what lives in our hearts, and at that moment, at the folly, I was so overcome with emotion, I couldn't speak. Literally, my love, I was struck completely dumb and the only outlet for my feelings was through passion. A raw, pulsing, primeval force, and when I saw that same love reciprocated in those lovely green eyes, I knew I had made a mistake.

I was wrong to have taken on Henry's stocks and his debts, and there was no time to explain.

I raced back to the solicitor's. The hell with Davenport's reputation! I intended to withdraw from the contract, as was my right. Henry was responsible for his own destruction. Not you, not me, not Lexie — yet we were the ones paying the price. Davenport gambled everything away, borrowing more heavily each time, knowing full well the house was falling into decay and neglect, and it was madness, using monies to prop up a name which he, and he alone, had fecklessly surrendered.

Meeting with you that afternoon, I saw everything clearly. I would divorce Cara, you would divorce Henry, and with the funds I'd had earmarked to settle his debts, I would support Lexie while she turned Lindale Manor around.

Ah, but with Henry, it was always the cheap option, wasn't it? Despite his oaths and his promises, his protestations to change, the only thing Henry Davenport cared about was himself.

Did he suspect I would change my mind? I'll never know. And maybe, my love, you would have spurned my proposal of marriage? I was too choked with emotion to ask. But you must believe me when I swear, with all my heart, that when I left you at the folly, you had never looked more beautiful. Or so happy.

Regrets are not in my nature, Lydia.

But if you do not reply to my letter, I will go to my grave with this one.

All my love, now and forever,

A.

Three days after posting that letter, baby Thomas was kidnapped.

CHAPTER 22

On second thoughts, Julia might have been a tad hasty in branding Cara an expert at suppressing emotions. When she finally tracked her down, it was in the Green Room, decanter in hand, pouring what was clearly not her first shot of whisky.

'Do you see that? Do you see that?' Julia followed Cara's shaking finger in the direction of an elaborate black and gold tower telephone, as far removed in elegance and complexity as you could get from the studio's basic stick arrangement. 'Why doesn't it ring? Why doesn't it ring and tell me they've found him? And what if they don't find him, eh? Suppose it drags on like last time?'

'They'll find him, Cara.'

'*Making every effort* — that's what the police said when they telephoned this morning. Exactly the same words they used in this same room eight years ago!' She ran to the window. Flung open the curtains. 'To hell with convention. To hell with people thinking I'm scared of a book-keeper. And after what that perfidious footman did, to hell with what might be splashed across the front page! What do you think it is this time? That I'm a punching bag? A doormat? A mouse? A fool?' She grabbed the decanter. Sank another straight shot.

'The spotlight will shift sooner than you think,' Julia said. Sensationalism had the lifespan of a mayfly. By the middle of next week, the paper would be back to its usual dull coverage of industrial achievements, political commentaries and doomsday predictions about how the rise in motorised vehicles would lead to congestion in the cities, bodily accidents, and worse. 'Didn't I read that the funeral is tomorrow?'

'It is, and you don't need me to tell you how much I'm dreading it.' Down went the third shot that Julia knew about, and still not half-past ten. 'His clerks are handling everything, can you believe that? They, and they alone apparently, are privy to the addresses to send the invitations, so while the widow dutifully responds to letters of condolence, strangers have been organising the readings, the hymns, the order of service. All as per Austin's instructions, I might add, right down to the coffin, the pall-bearers, even the flowers.'

Austin, Austin, always Austin.

'Well, let's see how much control he has now!'

Youth was on Julia's side. A twisted ankle was not. Fat chance of keeping pace with a wife who'd reached breaking point. By the time she caught up, Cara was standing motionless in the chapel doorway, staring at the polished oak coffin, lid open to reveal banks of padded ivory silk.

'Sophie's coffin was white,' she said so quietly that Julia strained to hear. 'White as the lilies that encircled it, and so small that they almost obscured it. Sunshine streamed through the stained-glass windows and danced on the lid. A lid that I insisted be closed, by the way. Screamed and shouted, until I got my own way.' She squared her shoulders. 'I couldn't have that tiny face looking up at me… At anyone…' Cara took three paces into the chapel. 'Then … then Arabella. After the most horrendous pregnancy, I was sick every day and, oh my God, twenty-five hours of labour —'

The smell of disinfectant and blood hadn't left her, she said. The cries for hot water. More towels. *Push! Push!* If it was a boy, Austin wanted to call him Thomas, but after a truly excruciating delivery, it was a girl. *Arabella*, he pronounced. *We shall call her Arabella, after my aunt.*

'Who cared what he called her! *Is she alive after that ordeal?* was all I wanted to know. I wouldn't let them leave her at the foot of the bed. *Bring the cot here. Next to me*, I said. *Closer!* They told me to sleep. *You're exhausted*, they said.' She moved another two steps towards her husband's coffin. 'When the midwife returned, I was in a deep, peaceful sleep. They said I had a smile on my face, and for that reason, they didn't wake me to tell me that my baby was dead. The child was gone, there was nothing anyone could do. Rest, they said. I'd need all my strength now to grieve.' Cara stepped up to the coffin and looked down. 'And then, of course, there was Thomas…'

For two minutes, Cara stared, and Julia hardly dared breathe. Then she picked up a candlestick, swung it high in the air, heedless of the hot, dripping wax. Julia rushed forward to stop her, but her arm was shaken off as Cara smashed at the lilies, every damned vase. She grabbed her again, but Cara's fury was relentless, and dammit, now she'd slipped in the water, helpless to stop the splintering, the smashing, the candle wax splashing. Helpless to stop Cara's pain.

Tears coursed down Julia's cheek. She knew Cara wanted to take that candlestick and smash Austin's face, except Austin Forbes was past feeling. So she vented her anger, her frustration, her fury, her pain at whatever was close, and it was only when her arms were too tired to swing that she let the candlestick drop. Hauling herself to her feet, Julia stared at the devastated pews. The wrecked hymn books and hassocks, the mangled lilies, broken glass, twisted candles.

At Austin, lying serene in his coffin. Triumphant to the end.

Cara had been quick to master her outburst in the chapel. A pinch of the lips, a few shuddering breaths, a clenching and unclenching of fists and *pff!* the mask was back as though it had never slipped. Discipline and control. Discipline and control. That was the glue that held her life together. Mustn't allow standards to slide! Back in the Green Room, she ordered coffee with the same mechanical precision that Julia noticed in the lists she'd drawn up. Not simply the checklist for her husband's bedroom, but the catalogue of mourning attire that widows were required to endure. Warm jackets for autumn, cashmere shawls for the winter, sufficient stiff black petticoats, and God knows how many cambric handkerchiefs with black borders. Two years is a long time to pass in mourning. In her position, more than most, one must be prepared, and the exactitude and planning Cara had put in was more than impressive.

With lists, there is order. With order, there is discipline. With discipline, there is control.

Austin drummed in that mantra to exert control, brainwashing her, like Julia's stepfather had brainwashed her mother, to the point where these women saw no other way. Even now, when he could never bully her again, Cara still rigidly stuck to the script, not yet seeing the irony.

That those lists were finally giving her back her control. Now she was the one making them. These were her choices, not his.

Maybe Austin wasn't so triumphant after all.

'I've decided.' Cara stared into her coffee. 'I shall be leaving the day after the funeral.'

'Are you sure you're not rushing this?'

Julia's stomach had flipped at her mother's haste to re-marry. The workhouse would have been ten times — a hundred times

— better than the hell they had to put up with, but money, she supposed, would have cushioned it.

'You can call it running away, if you like. The press undoubtedly will call it history repeating itself, *Mrs. Forbes not facing up to her responsibilities, exactly as she did when she left her husband to mourn alone after their daughters died*, but I simply couldn't stay under the same roof as Austin back then, and now?' Cara swallowed. 'Once again, our tragedies are being played out on the front pages. Once it goes to trial, they'll dredge up my darling dead daughters, and that terrible night eight years ago, forcing me to re-live the fear, the uncertainty and, most cruelly of all, making me re-live the hope.' Cara closed her eyes. 'The only thing I've ever wanted is to be left alone with my grief, and as long as I remain in this house, I'll never find peace.'

'You can't outrun heartache, Cara.' *Trust me, I know.*

'Maybe not, but it won't stop me trying. After Sophie died, I took the first train to Italy, and spent the summer on the Isle of Capri. Does that make me a bad mother? Possibly. Probably. I don't know, and to be frank with you, Julia, I don't care. All I knew was, I couldn't face staying in the house where my baby had died.'

'You don't need to explain.'

'Yes. Yes, I do. I need to explain why I can't sleep, can't focus, can't go back inside Austin's room, because unless you understand, you'll think me hard and unfeeling.'

'I doubt that.'

But Cara was lost in her pain. 'After that traumatic birth with Arabella, I was too weak to escape, but once I was strong enough … indeed, the *instant* I was strong enough, I went to Switzerland. Lake Geneva. The air, they told me, was clean.' She exhaled. 'After Thomas was taken, which was very different of course, I rented a house in Provence, and maybe I *am* irresponsible, maybe I *am* a coward, but one thing I know is that every minute of every day I waited for the telegram that would tell me they'd found him. One way or the other.'

'Why did you come back? If you were so unhappy in this house, why not stay in Provence?'

'Austin fetched me,' she said.

Nothing else to be said.

CHAPTER 23

Chief Superintendent Blaine lifted the lid of his kiln-dried, Spanish cedar wood humidor and carefully considered the contents. Aficionados generally agree that the morning should be reserved for smaller and milder cigars, upgrading to a medium strength in the afternoon, and saving the large, full-bodied beasts until after dinner, where they could be savoured at leisure. The hell with protocol. Blaine picked out a fat, dark, Cuban Bolivar, sliced off the cap with a clean snip of the cutter, then pushed his half-specs back up his nose and re-read the report from DI Collingwood, which said he was following several reliable leads on the cat burglar and was close to breaking the case.

'Close to breaking, my arse.'

If he was that close, he wouldn't bother typing a report, which meant the bastard was up to something, and Blaine knew exactly what that something was.

Rotating the Bolivar's foot round the flame of his lighter, he inhaled the cigar's peppery, slightly coffee, aroma. Once it was alight, he gently peeled off the band, then leaned back in his swivel chair. If anyone bothered to look past the fat bloke in the swivel chair — beyond the mess of box files and folders, the piles of papers on his desk, the dust and ash — they'd see a police officer who'd risen through the ranks on merit, not by sucking up or greasing palms, and certainly not by cutting corners! A man who'd followed every one of Robert Peel's principles with grit and determination, because he believed these were as right and fitting as God's own ten Commandments.

Still. *Could* he have missed something eight years ago? Throughout it all, one quote from the *Broadhurst Gazette* never left him.

Mrs. Forbes has remained indoors throughout the ordeal. Looking drawn and pale, the only comment she has made to the press has been, 'God will take care of my son, I just know it.' We all pray she is right.

Blaine put his feet on the desk, puffing slowly so as not to overheat the cigar and spoil its flavour. He wasn't vindictive by nature, but he hoped to God whoever took that boy rotted in hell. He lived that nightmare alongside the Forbes, befriending the workforce, sweet-talking the maids, mateying up with the migrants. Month after month, as uncertainty dragged on, he hadn't let up. For God's sake, a child was missing! Scared and alone, crying for his mummy? Or cold and buried under the earth? Blaine's dedication to that investigation cost him his marriage, but by Christ, so help him God, he'd do the same thing all over again.

Tempting as it was to write Collingwood off as a sanctimonious know-it-all, who believed his chief superintendent thought scruples were the dangly bits at the back of the throat that a surgeon takes out when you're six, Blaine knew better. His DI was ambitious and smart, with bloody good instincts — but he hadn't been there. He might *imagine* the impact. It's not the same as living through it. A whole town was torn apart, and the wounds had only just started to heal.

He rolled the cigar between his thumb and index finger, studying the pattern of the overlapping leaves, the way they all spiralled in the same direction, with just the lightest of sheen. It was said that every hand-rolled Havana went through two hundred and twenty-two different processes before it was ready to be smoked. The type of man who enjoys such cigars appreciates that level of care and attention. Blaine hadn't missed one damn thing eight years ago, on that, he'd bet his life. He was buggered if he'd re-open the kidnap.

With a snort, he ripped open the envelope Collingwood had clipped to his report on the cat burglar and pulled out the handwritten note. Better not be his bloody resignation. Pain in the arse or not, when he was on form, few officers could —

'*I do realise, sir, that the Forbes murder is not my case,*' the note read. '*However, book-keepers are generally unaccustomed to sleeping rough, yet no food has been reported stolen, or barns broken into, even after four days on the run. I therefore feel it would be remiss of me not to convey my conclusion that Mr. Higgins has an accomplice.*' Damn. He *was* on bloody form!

Blaine's feet shot off the desk as he reached for the telephone. 'Get me Inspector Collingwood at Boot Street.'

'You're positive you searched every square inch of Austin's room, Julia? Checked his pockets, his pillows, any secret compartments in his writing desk?' Collingwood swore he'd only dropped by to remind Julia to be careful out there — and all right, yes, maybe check on Billy, whistling *How much is that doggy in the window?* while he slapped varnish on the woodwork. And very well, as she insisted, he'd stopped to have a quick bite to eat. Only the instant he saw those full, heavy breasts fighting the injustice of their silk imprisonment, he said, he'd felt obligated to free them, and for Julia's part, surely it was her civic duty to let the long arm of the law take its course? A deliciously long, slow arm as it happened, but from the moment he first pulled her to him, right back when she was his prime suspect for multiple murders, and their lips locked until neither of them could breathe, she hadn't looked at another man.

'Detective Inspector Collingwood, does it look like I'm hiding anything?'

Grey eyes raked Julia's nakedness. 'In the interests of thoroughness, it's my duty to make sure.'

'Again?'

'Afraid so, miss. Turn round, hands on the wall, please.'

Julia told herself the arrangement was casual. No more than a sharing of pleasure, and a much-needed release for them both, and it was true. As his heart pounded beneath the palm of her hand, she craved the taste of his skin every bit as much as he longed to explore every crevice and inch of her body. Two people finding redemption in mutual satisfaction. What was the problem with that? But she knew exactly what the problem was. With a wife who'd used sex as a weapon from their wedding night, mistresses came with the territory, but the very word mistress implied a relationship, and that was the one thing they couldn't have.

He was a policeman.

She'd taken life in cold blood.

The quicker she ended this … arrangement, the better. Keep it professional from now on.

Unfortunately, logic and lust make for bad company. Detective Inspector Collingwood brought out an intensity that Julia hadn't known or imagined, and once the butterfly's out of the chrysalis, there's no going back.

Selfish? Perhaps.

Reckless? Beyond doubt.

Dangerous? You bet your life.

But right now, in her studio, tangled in the heat, the excitement, the madness beside the very backdrop where Lexie had posed, Julia watched the same fire that burned in her belly reflect in John Collingwood's eyes. Like the lost souls who haunt opium dens, they both needed more.

How would it end? Badly, of course. But while it lasted —?

While it lasted, the world could go to hell in a handcart.

CHAPTER 24

'Blimey!' Billy's jaw dropped. 'Look at all them bangers.'

Hangers? Clangers? Julia followed his gaze. 'Oh. Sausages.'

Strings and strings of them. Smoked, dried, studded with crispy black peppercorns, salami reeking of garlic. Fat ones, thin ones, long ones, short ones, all dangling from hooks on a pole stretched across the window above hams of every shape and size, along with lobes of duck and goose liver that were raw, cooked, somewhere between, chopped, or turned into pâté and served, sliced, from earthenware dishes.

'It's like being back in Soho!'

'Herr Schultz.' Julia waved to the big German, swabbing shiny blue and white tiles with a dishcloth. Acknowledgement came in a show of teeth under a moustache so wide and so thick that a nest of rodents could happily live there without anyone noticing. 'He opened his delicatessen two weeks ago and commissioned a photo to celebrate the occasion, him and the family lined up outside. Because the set-up costs left him strapped for cash, we agreed on payment in kind.'

Inside, his wife sliced cheese which was more holes than anything else, and weighed it on a set of bronze scales. Behind the counter, jars of quince paste and onion jams balanced like circus display teams on racks, alongside glass jars full of the spices that accompanied them. Peppercorns, bay, and tiny dried redcurrants.

'Must be nice to have mates.' Billy shot her his signature grin as Julia emerged five minutes later. ''Specially when they could be related to Prince Albert, God rest his mortal soul.'

'You mean you *don't* have royal friends?'

He relieved her of the basket, weighed down with enough luxuries to give a wild stallion gout. 'Don't have friends, full stop. Can't make 'em if you're not round long enough to put down roots, and you can't put down roots when your trade's all about inspecting grass on the other side of the fence.'

'There's no law against dropping anchor, Billy, and who knows. If you try it, you might even like it.' Telling lies, keeping secrets, unable to trust anyone wasn't simply exhausting. It was the loneliest road ever walked.

'Talkin' of trades, Miss Photographer Lady, is it true?' She'd forgotten how good he was when it came to the changing of subjects. 'You take pictures of stiffs, dontcha?'

Julia laughed. 'Accounts for half my business and a fraction of the income, because look around, Billy. Tell me what you see.'

The same twist of the mouth, she imagined, that he'd give when humouring a patient in the local asylum. 'Narrow streets. Cobblestones. Coffee shops. Chemists shops. Half-timbered houses —'

'I meant the people.'

'Which ones? The fancy ladies swishing their fancy scalloped hems? Or the toffs in silk cravats, twirling their Indian rosewood canes?'

'Both. Because these are the ones who can afford family portraits by the bucket load, but over there —' she jabbed a finger in the direction of the smoke that shrouded the town — 'the women on the other side of the canal don't have wardrobes bursting with lacy tea gowns, or hats that cost six months' wages.' They don't even have wardrobes, full stop. From factory hands to dockers, costermongers to the workers in the opium dens, cloth caps and linen aprons were the order of the day, along with suits worn into holes that only came out on Sundays, and bonnets for practicality, rather than show. 'They're the ones who need *memento mori*, Billy.' The only photos they'd ever have of husbands, wives or children, and so what if they were dead? 'Precious memories for them to treasure, and I refuse to charge more than they can afford.'

In fact, the words "sodding" "great" and "loss" sprang to mind. Especially given the amount of time it took to secure the deceased in a natural position, arranging their clothes, their hair, painting their faces to make them appear lifelike, and all the props and paraphernalia involved.

'I meant police work. Murder. Stuff like that. That's your job, innit?'

'I've recorded a couple of crime scenes, yes.' Swerving to avoid a matron coming out of the cake shop with a box tied with red ribbon, Julia's eye was drawn to the fruit laid out in front of the greengrocer's. Eight years ago these would have been Davenport pippins and Davenport plums. Quality that was still talked about today. 'The latest was three days ago. Austin Forbes. You know about that?'

'Nope.'

'Bigwig from Broadhurst, but killed in Boot Street's jurisdiction at a local beauty spot. The police know who shot him, and the killer's on the run, but Austin was such a pig that half the population of Broadhurst had motive, means and opportunity, and normally I wouldn't care that he'd been put down like a dog.'

'But?'

She paused outside the taxidermist's, trying not to meet the accusing glare of the Arctic fox cub, or the defiance in the toucan's glass eye. 'For one thing, no one deserves to die the way he did, and for another his son was kidnapped, and, despite paying the ransom, which wasn't even picked up, that was the last he saw of his baby.'

'Poor bugger.' Billy shook his head. 'Me, at least I got a grave to visit. Not that I do, mind. Hurts too bloody much. But the point is, I got one. What sort of monster snatches a kid, then keeps his old man dangling year after year?'

'What do you do with the money?' Julia asked him.

'What money?'

'Don't play games with me, Billy.' He positioned himself at the station, knowing that going on holiday, taking day trips, or visiting family makes people better disposed to toss a coin in his cap. Or, like with her at the post-box, by pointing out that a halfpenny's the price of the stamp they were posting would result in the chinking of coppers. Julia bet this "poor, half-blind, homeless soldier" was earning the same as a slop worker or a girl on the telegraph, if not more. 'You make a fortune from plucking heart strings.'

Yet if was living the life of riley, the dirt wouldn't be so ingrained, and his eyes wouldn't be half so haunted.

He opened his mouth to make a joke and change the subject. Then met the glare in Julia's eye. 'Kids.' He'd shifted the basket to his other hand, back again, then repeat. But eventually it came tumbling out. The children — orphans, runaways, abandoned, take your pick — all too young, too sick or too injured to work, who were reduced to scavenging the streets or trawling through waste, starving, limping and cold. 'I don't give 'em the coins I get, though.'

'You buy food.'

'And blankets. And clothes. I buy 'em toy trains and dolls, too, but yeah. Mostly food, and that's why I keep moving. Can't let the little buggers become reliant on me, 'cause where does it end? Like dogs, they start followin' yer. Think that 'cause they're close by, they'll get priority, but it ain't for me to decide, is it? Not when there's scores of the poor sods round the slums, along the canal, out by the factories, sleeping rough in places where they won't be picked on, robbed, beaten, or raped.'

Oh, Billy. Billy, Billy, Billy. You couldn't save your wife, you couldn't save your unborn child, and you know damn well you can't save even half these kids.

Was there anywhere, *anywhere*, Julia thought, to escape the death of a child?

Running a bath when she got home (her ankle was killing her), Julia asked herself, in what way was taking Thomas different from keeping her stepfather's family dangling? Didn't they deserve a grave to weep over, too? Tipping in a handful of lavender salts and swishing them round to dissolve them, the answer was categorically "no". To a man, they knew what that bastard was like. Angry, resentful, blaming everyone but himself for two years in the military prison at Aldershot, before finishing the last year of his sentence in Pentonville as part of his dishonourable discharge. Bitter that he came home with his tail between his legs, instead of a hero carried high through the streets on their shoulders. Uncaring that he'd infected his wife with syphilis, inflicting sores and ulcers on her, and God knows what else, and they knew damn well that he took his resentment out at the end of his fists. Fists that were no match for a stick of a wife, a boy too small and too soft for his age, and a girl whose kitten he strangled to show her who's boss.

Julia tied up her hair and slipped out of her clothes, folding them neatly over the chair. Not every member of that family was a drunk and a wife-beater, but every drunkard and wife-beater she'd known came from that family. Even by their

171

standards, they regretted the rotten apple in their midst, but instead of helping the vulnerable and defenceless, they closed ranks.

Well, no one was going to close ranks on Cara. Not while Julia had a say in it.

She sank into the water, steam swirling round the mirror and obscuring the glass. Even in his polished oak coffin lined with ivory silk, Austin still had presence. Thanks to chiselled cheekbones and sharp pointed chin, his jaw remained strong despite middle age, his mouth firm, and his waxed pencil moustache no doubt matched the shine on his shoes. Cara mightn't be weeping buckets over her husband, but a lot of ladies, she suspected, would.

Controlling bastard or not, to cope with the kidnappers, the police and the press, he'd been forced to mask his grief, too. What odds that the longer it dragged on, the deeper he'd had to bury those feelings? How challenging was that, for a man who, for the first time in his life, found there were things beyond even his rigid control? Things like justice. Revenge. Even the comfort of knowing what happened to his son was denied him, hardening what passed for a heart into granite.

And how did the horror of that night compare to the terror of dragging his bullet-riddled body through the grass, while his killer stalked him like game?

Whatever anyone's opinion of Austin Forbes, he'd spared no effort to track down his son. Whether that stemmed from a need for control, a determination not to be thwarted by kidnappers, or a genuine love for his boy Julia had no idea. In any case, it was beside the point. He'd thrown every ounce of his wealth, power and reputation to discover the truth, but for all his influence, it had not brought him justice.

For all his money, it had not brought his son home.

And for all his faults, he'd suffered the unspeakable pain of losing a child and died without knowing the fate of his son.

Perhaps death, in its own way, was a kindness?

CHAPTER 25

'Blaine didn't swallow your line about closing in on the cat burglar, then.' Sergeant Charlie Kincaid perched on the edge of the desk, while Collingwood hung the earpiece back in its hook.

'Let's say his language nearly melted the telephone.'

'We've put the fear of God into every fence within a five-mile radius, doesn't that constitute close?'

'Only if something turned up, but bugger, Charlie. Not a brooch, not a ring, not so much as a snuff box.'

'He's a sneaky bastard, remember.' Kincaid packed his pipe bowl with tobacco. 'Only steals stuff that people won't notice for a while and gives him some breathing space, so maybe that's his game? He wants you to think he's smarter than you.'

'He is.'

'You're just pissed, because you're itching to set your size twelves in Broadhurst and this little sod's in the way.'

'There's more than one way to skin a cat, Charlie.' Hence his note to Blaine attached to his report, saying he realised it wasn't his case, but after four days on the run, didn't it seem odd that no one had reported any food stolen or barns broken into? 'Book-keepers aren't accustomed to sleeping rough. Some activity should have manifested itself by now.'

'The implication being that someone's hiding him?'

'Mrs. McAllister is pretty sure that "that someone" is the lovely Lexie, but I can't tell Blaine without tipping my hand. What I did say was that if Ezra knows the game's up, then the funeral is the perfect opportunity to make his move.'

'You mean, if he's going to hang, might as well be for a sheep as a lamb?' Kincaid lit his pipe and puffed. 'That doesn't fit with what we know of Higgins.'

'No, but it pulls a lot of men away from the manhunt.'

'I take it back.' Kincaid's laugh could have passed for water down a blocked sink. 'The burglar's not the only sneaky bastard round here.'

'Whatever leverage Lexie is using to manipulate him, I'll bet my pension he'll use that window tomorrow to see his wife and baby.'

'Exactly how do you propose to catch him, when you're banned from Broadhurst? Because killer or not, John, he's not worth you losing your job over.'

'Agreed.'

Collingwood stood up and reached for his hat. If he told Charlie his plan, Charlie would stop him. But then, Charlie had never buried a child.

'You know, I *thought* I heard the clop of a hansom.' Lydia was swinging a flat wicker basket along the path round the lake at Lindale Manor when Julia caught up with her. As she'd expected, not a crease in Lydia's skirt, not a blonde hair out of place!

'I came to drop off Lexie's portrait.'

More accurately, she'd come to force Lexie's hand. Like she'd told Cara, sensationalism was the mayfly of the media. Once it dies, leads peter out, clues run dry, and without proof, the suspicions of a mere woman (even if Mrs. McAllister was a police crime scene photographer) weren't going to convince Blaine to re-open the kidnap. And with Cara still hell-bent on outrunning her heartache, any hope of finding answers would vanish like smoke in the wind.

'How's the ankle?' Lydia asked.

'I'm hoping a walk will strengthen it, and since Lexie said you were on a blackberry hunt, I thought you might need a hand.'

'I need the company more, truth be told.'

'It's not easy being the second horse in the harness, is it?'

Lydia laughed. 'I'd forgotten how annoyingly perceptive you are, but you're right. Lexie and I have been pulling together since Henry died, but poverty, I'm afraid, demands isolation. I cannot deny that the claustrophobia is crushing.'

Passing behind a bed of blue hydrangeas, the path disappeared almost at once. Manicured sophistication gave way to untamed nature, where hawthorn and elm blocked out the sky, and birches and plane trees rubbed roots with ferns and broad-leaved helleborines.

'A firm favourite with Parisian beggars, this stuff.' Lydia rippled her fingers through the foam of wild clematis that was trailing through the whole tangle. 'They rub their skin with it until they break out in sores. More sympathy, that way. Bigger handouts.'

Beggars who could use a tip or two from Billy Briggs!

Navigating arching thorns from the dog roses and roots that just ached to trip a girl up, Julia was relieved when the woods finally opened into a clearing. She wouldn't exactly say she felt uneasy out here. But without doubt, it was the sort of place where, if anything happened, no one would find her for some time. Then a church bell rang in the distance, and instead of relief, ice ran down her spine. These were the same woods that backed on to the beauty spot where Austin was killed.

'True love is a rare find.' Julia's voice was commendably steady. 'When your soul mate dies, the loss must be devastating.'

Lydia looked at the sky. Smoothed her skirts with the palms of her hands. 'The best blackberries are over —'

'But is that loss devastating, as in overwhelming,' Julia persisted, 'or devastating, as in destructive?'

Lydia turned. Pursed her lips. 'All I can tell you, dear, is that, at the time, the pain is so raw, it's not a question of not being able to think straight. You can't think at all.'

'Are we talking about Henry?' Julia paused. 'Or his tycoon neighbour?'

Credit where it's due, Lydia's composure barely slipped. 'Please don't be offensive.'

'I know about you and Austin.'

There was barely a heartbeat's pause. 'There should be chestnuts dropping around now, as well. We usually roast them in the fire, but Cook likes to boil them with syrup to candify for the winter, or turn them into thick, creamy soup.'

'Lydia, stop! I've read the letters. They were hidden away in his room.'

'Then you'll know that that's more than I ever did. I returned them unopened, every last one, and what of it? This is ancient history.'

'Your affair ended the day Henry killed himself.'

'I have nothing to say on the matter, and that's final.'

'Suit yourself, I know it all anyway.' A soft breeze hissed through the yellowing leaves. Magpies chattered in the branches. 'Vivacious, enlightened, lovely young woman marries into landed gentry. Her stepdaughter brands her a gold-digger, set on overthrowing the current regime by giving her husband a male heir, but ten years pass, and no sign of a son. Who knows? Was the second wife barren? Was the husband taking his pleasure elsewhere —?'

'Tosh! I had no intention of cutting Lexie out of anything, in fact, that was the best thing about my marriage. Henry was no longer in the first flush of youth, and having raised Lexie to take over, he didn't want a tribe of children running round. As for me, I didn't want children at all. Are you shocked?'

Julia doubted anything would shock her when it came to the Davenport women. 'Are you saying it was a love match?'

'If you're suggesting I was one of those girls who engaged in a loveless marriage purely for financial security, the desire for a roof over my head, and the satisfaction of status, nothing could be more debasing.'

'I rather think I was asking if you loved each other.'

'At the beginning, Henry might have loved me. But unless you met him, you couldn't know what he was like. He was a — *bon viveur* I suppose is the phrase. Witty, amusing, exceedingly dashing.' Lydia leaned in to pick a handful of plump, juicy blackberries. Julia held out the basket. Lydia laid them gently on the wicker, filling the air with their dense, fruity aroma. 'After he died, Lexie and I discovered we both wanted the same thing. Freedom, without being accountable to anyone but ourselves.'

'Different standards for the two sexes is the curse of our society.'

'Why can't people accept the concept of equality? Embrace it, even? Why do the majority of women continue to spurn independence, while men view the notion as radical nonsense?'

'A lot of men feel threatened by strong women.'

'Is that the voice of experience speaking?' With a wry smile, Lydia moved on to the next bush. 'Needless to say, Lexie took to estate management like a duck to water. Me, I was too busy revelling in liberation and freedom to see how feckless my husband had become, and since I didn't marry him for his money, I could hardly complain when it ran out.'

'Your love for him — what? Faded away?'

'Eroded. There's a difference. The trouble with *bon viveurs*, you see, is that the fascination with new toys quickly wears off. I could never compete with the breathless thrill of a spinning roulette wheel, or the roll of the dice, or cards landing face up, and that's where Austin fitted in. Two lost, lonely people finding solace in a time of mutual need, if you like, but in spite of everything, Julia, every damn thing that happened since, I regret nothing.'

Really? Because that wasn't how Austin's letters came over.

CHAPTER 26

The stone tower stood in solitary splendour.

Built purely for effect, a means to broadcast its owner's status and wealth, it stood twenty feet high, was circular in design, and resembled some kind of ruined fortification, without any military function. Julia flattened herself against the wall. In her hand was a British Bull Dog five-shot revolver, poised to fire every damned round. Her mouth was dry as she peered round the doorway.

It took a few seconds to adjust to the gloom, but wherever Higgins was holed up, thick dust on the spiral staircase proved it wasn't here. No traces of food. No traces of bedding. No traces of human activity. She slipped the revolver into her reticule and leaned her back against the folly, absorbing the heat from the stone.

This was where the money was left. Where Henry trysted with Lydia.

The epicentre of pretty much everything.

If she could figure out why the ransom wasn't collected, she'd have the answer to Thomas's kidnap. But right now, all Julia could think of was a little boy's sobs.

And the pounding of his terrified heart.

'Wine's on the terrace, Julia,' Lexie called. 'Lydia has a headache, Grace doesn't drink, so it's just you, me, and this claret.'

'Lydia has nothing of the sort and Grace is varnishing the banisters, no doubt wearing gloves, on the grounds that well-heeled suitors find calluses and splinters off-putting.'

'Nothing gets past you, does it?' Lexie laughed. 'This way.'

The setting sun, slanting through the trees, peppered the table with bright orange beams.

'All this slog and hard graft, it's for your daughter, isn't it?'

'The clock's ticking, Julia. She needs to find a husband, and to snare a good one she needs a dowry. I can't have Society thinking that she's a pauper.'

'Hence your concentrating on the principal reception rooms, gardens and entrance.'

'First impressions are crucial, and once I've drawn up a list of suitors, it's important that their eyes pop out on stalks when they see Lindale. Inside, as well as out.' Lexie poured wine into two crystal glasses. 'Should they happen to make assumptions about what is beyond their line of vision, that's hardly my fault, and if it means painting over the *chinois* décor, then so be it. I prefer the modern idea of light, uncluttered rooms, anyway.'

'I've never been a fan of *rococo*, either,' Julia admitted. 'Bringing *art nouveau* to the Manor would be a breath of fresh air.' Shame Lexie wouldn't be around to breathe it.

Sunset turned the lake to molten gold. A soft breeze tickled the trees, but the air remained sultry. A fox loped home with a rabbit.

'Grace has no idea what you're planning, has she?'

'I'm saving the heart-to-heart until we're close to hosting balls and *soirées*. In the meantime, the best thing I can give my daughter is her freedom.'

'The longer you leave it, the more she'll resent you.'

'She'll resent poverty and spinsterhood a hell of a lot more!' Lexie paused. 'Love isn't all it's cracked up to be, anyhow, though I really should instruct her in the social graces expected of a girl of her standing.'

'Like how pinning her hair up is just as important when it comes to meeting visitors as slipping into sumptuous watered silk tea gowns?'

'Do you know, I'm so used to those damned braids that I hadn't even noticed?' Lexie sighed. 'I was thinking more about pointing out to her how that particular silk number is a Charles Worth, then reminding her how much the bloody thing cost, and that covering it with cat hairs and snags from little sharp claws isn't how society women go about business. Unfortunately, there are always more pressing calls on my time.'

'Like guests putting holes in your floor?'

'Three more dust motes, and the blasted thing would have collapsed anyway.'

Julia studied her across the rim of her wine glass. 'Have you considered hiring a second handyman to speed things along? There's only so much one boy can do on his own.'

Behind them, the sun was sinking in a ball of bright red fury. Noisy crows flew home to their roosts.

'I can't afford to take on another labourer, and Dickon isn't exactly on his own. As you discovered, he has three female assistants to call on, and for the record, he isn't a boy, he's a man.'

Indeed he was. One whose muscles punched through his open-necked shirt, whose hair fell over one eye, who Julia saw slip out of Lexie's bedroom, tucking that same shirt into his trousers, when she'd used the excuse of the water closet to take another snoop round. Because, she had reasoned, if Ezra wasn't in the folly, maybe they were just bold enough to hide him in the house? Maybe it was him, and not Lydia or a servant, that Julia heard, sobbing in the dark?

'I'm not sure this will help you clear your name,' Julia said slowly, 'but the police are wondering if they haven't got the kidnap back to front.' *Warfare is based on deception and planning,* Lexie had said. So she could hardly complain when truth was one of the casualties! 'That money wasn't the motive, and Thomas was taken to get back at Austin.'

There was an uncharacteristically long pause. 'Why would anyone do that?'

'Hell hath no fury springs to mind.' Julia sniffed the wine. 'And I'm getting the impression that a lot of women in Austin's life have been scorned.'

This time the pause was even longer. 'Is that a fact.'

'You tell me.' The wine was rich, and full-bodied. 'You were one of his conquests.'

Bloomer suits didn't lend themselves to the concealment of bulky correspondence, but there had been just about room to secrete Austin's last emotional outpouring to Lydia. The rest of the letters Julia had returned to their secret compartment, to collect later. Apart from one. Written to him, not from him, this was one of the pieces of paper that Julia had found inside the wallet taped to the underside of the desk. Paper that was covered in bold, free flowing, female writing.

'What I don't understand, Lexie, is why. He robbed you of your land, your father, your income and your future. You were aware that he browbeat his wife, bullied his workforce, screwed his creditors, and slept with any woman who let him. Yet you happily went to his bed.'

'Oh my gosh, that was a long time ago —'

'It was last month.' In his desk, Julia had found a receipt for a suite at The Langham, London's first purpose-built grand hotel, and the largest. 'I don't know when it began, but that's the day your affair ended.'

Once again this was guesswork, based on the fact that there no more recent transactions, but spoken with such confidence that Julia could almost see the dilemma behind those artless, blue eyes. Was the police spy bluffing or not? *The biggest mistake we can make now is losing Julia's trust.* Lexie tossed a mental coin that landed truth up.

'For seven and a half years, it kept eating away at me. Why Papa signed away every damned thing that the Davenports stood for. I thought … if I seduced Austin, shared intimacies with him, got him to trust me, he would give me an explanation.'

'Except he'd given your father his word instead.'

'What good's that? What good's honour, when it destroys people's lives!' Lexie sank the rest of her wine in one gulp. 'I'll be honest. My heart would turn somersaults at the mere thought of our trysts.' She smiled sheepishly. 'Of Austin taking me down to dinner on his arm, ordering champagne, and knowing that afterwards he'd be licking that same champagne from the dip in my collarbone. In fact, the hardest thing was what he kept below his waist, but dammit, I still deserved to know. He *owed* me that. Why every damn thing was taken from me! As a last resort, I resolved to provoke him into an explanation, during the course of which I said a lot of totally inexcusable things. Which you know, since you've obviously read the apology I wrote him, and I meant every word, Julia. Truly.'

The sun disappeared. The terrace was swallowed by darkness.

'But still Austin wouldn't budge. He'd broken his oath once, he said, and he was damned if he'd do it again, then calmed me down the way he did best.' Lexie let out an involuntary shiver that had nothing to do with the cooling night air. 'I'll tell you the reason I ended the affair, and it had nothing to do with my outburst, or Austin's refusal to tell me what happened.' Silence twisted the air. 'It was because, when he climaxed that afternoon, Austin called out a name. And that name wasn't mine.'

'It was Lydia's.'

'How —?' The colour drained from Lexie's face. 'How could you possibly know that?'

Leaves whispered. Crickets rasped in the grass.

'Because I know everything.' Julia stood up. 'I know how the cat burglar operates, I know who kidnapped Thomas, I know where Ezra fits in, and I know why Austin was murdered.'

'But —?'

'I can't prove it.'

Time was running out. Julia needed to force Lexie's hand. What better way than to blast a cannon ball through that wall of complacency when she was vulnerable? Then follow straight up by leaving?

'Dickon will drive you home, I insist.'

The ploy worked. Lexie's voice was shaky. She kept wiping her palms down the side of her skirts. Her face was whiter than the porcelain you could read those tax demands through. In fact, Julia was still feeling smug when Dickon turned up a few minutes later in the sporty, stylish, single-horse carriage that Lexie kept expressly to prove to Society that the Davenports were still influential and rich. A conceit that lasted right up to the moment Julia noticed the familiarity with which he sat in the driving seat, and the ease with which he held the reins. Unease rippled up her spine.

For a workman, he spent an awful lot of time leaning against outside walls, ankles crossed, thumbs looped in his waistband, for all the world a young man taking a well-earned break. Yet even in the short amount of time Julia had spent at Lindale, she'd noticed that the instant the window above him closed, or the open door next to him was bolted, he'd lift his head, sending a hank of dark hair over one eye which he made no effort to push away, and casually saunter off. Proof that a man can hear anything around here … providing he knows where to stand.

In other words, the blackmail was either an ongoing process, in which case Lexie's sleeping with him was part of the payment … or she was using him as her partner in crime.

'How exciting, mind if I sit with you?' Julia breezed, jumping up alongside him without waiting for an answer.

Whether Dickon was part of this sordid business or not, if any loaded barrels happened to be waving around, a passenger in the back seat made for easy pickings. Sitting beside the driver, on the other hand, ensured that a spray of pellets was just as likely to hit him. A situation she could take advantage of by artlessly engaging him in conversation. By which she meant, suck him dry.

It was only after the phaeton turned through the gates that Julia realised her mistake.

Unease turned to cold fear.

Not only did the sultry Mr. Tyler turn out to be the sort of a chap who won't use ten words when none will do, she'd underestimated just how many isolated spots there were between Lindale and Oakbourne. At least Dickon had seen her revolver in action and knew she was armed.

'You told Lexie *what?*' Collingwood asked Julia when she was safely back home.

'Photographs, Inspector, require the sitter to remain still for at least the half-second it takes to release the shutter.' Julia's voice was muffled by the heavy cover as she lined up her shot. 'Twisting your head like an owl who's just heard a mouse in the undergrowth isn't what I would class motionless.'

'This is a waste of time, Julia.' Collingwood jumped up. 'Just tell me why —'

'My time or yours?'

'Both. Your idea of hanging portraits of the officers on the station walls is —'

'Inspired?'

'— well-intentioned, but completely misguided.'

Julia's idea was simple. Police stations are cold, scary, intimidating places, even to felons. Imagine what it was like for anxious law-abiding citizens, coming in to report missing wives, missing children, missing property, missing cats, or whatever else they reported. By seeing instantly who they were dealing with, being able to put names to faces and know they weren't alone, the public could then identify with individual police officers, and the distance between the two sides would shrink. Once community spirit started to knit, it would be very hard for the Top Brass to close Boot Street down. What could Inspector Collingwood possibly have against that?

'I may have my faults, John, but being wrong isn't one of them. Now sit down and try to look like the man who puts the fear of God into scoundrels and thieves, rather than the man who is just beginning to understand what it feels like to have blood running through his veins, instead of alcohol.'

'It'll look worse than a line of mugshots.'

'Only if you keep that expression up.'

'Just tell me why you came out with that ridiculous bluff,' he was saying.

'Have you stopped to consider that it might be true?'

'Christ, Julia.' Collingwood threw his arms in the air. 'Why don't you pin a target on your back and be done with?'

'Lexie won't hurt me.'

'No. She gets other people to do her dirty work.'

'Agreed, but I'm here, aren't I?'

'You say you want to force Lexie's hand, well, I already have. I sent the chief super a note mentioning that since Austin's funeral will be at St. Michael's instead of Chislehurst Hall, Ezra Higgins might take the opportunity to exact revenge. If the only way to bring her to justice means falling on the sword of my career, then so be it. He'll pull half his men from the search to protect Cara. The other half he'll have lying in wait, in case Higgins calls on his wife and baby instead.'

'What am I missing here, John?' Blaine could hardly claim Collingwood was inserting himself in the case, when the decision was his. 'He's not going to sack you over one paltry suggestion. An unofficial suggestion at that.'

'Agreed.' Collingwood's grey eyes stared into the distance. She had a feeling they were staring into the past. At a daughter who did not deserve to die. 'Even going behind his back might not sway it. The nail in the coffin is when he finds out it was a ruse to get his men out of the way. That's why I couldn't tell Charlie. If Blaine suspects Charlie is privy to the plan, he'll toss him out on his ear, too. Starting at first light, when every officer in Broadhurst is either at the church or surrounding the Higgins house, I'll have a team of dogs out.'

'But that's excellent! With the heat off Ezra Higgins, my bluff will push Lexie to silence the only man who can hang her, except your dogs will track him down before she can make her move.'

'If only.' Collingwood's mouth turned down. 'Dogs will sniff out a corpse.'

CHAPTER 27

'— *commit this body to the ground, for dust thou art, and unto dust shalt thou return* —'

Julia stole a glance at Cara, staring stoically ahead through the heavy fabric of her weeping-veil. As befitting their status, the male servants from Chislehurst Hall were kitted out in heavy crêpe trimming and black kidskin gloves. The women wore black bonnets hung with black ribbon. For the life of her, Julia couldn't understand why widows were forced to wear black for a year. Sod respect, and sod Queen Victoria's exemplary standards, as well. Did no one see — did no one care — that it isolated them, and isolation was the last thing they needed? All this business about bombazine, Henrietta cloth, Melrose and astrakhan, the so-called staples of mourning wear, and sleeves needed to be fitted with extra wide cuffs so (oh please!) widows could blow their noses with discretion when they burst into tears? Did no one see — did no one care — how demeaning this was? Never mind the torture of her son's disappearance, this was Cara's third time through the wringer of bereavement. Hadn't she been shut out enough?

'— *ring this bell to mark our brother's passing, as we join in silent prayer to bid him safe journey* —'

Broadhurst had also been caught on the hop by the new venue for the funeral, reducing gossips and rubber-neckers to a trickle. Even the press, bar one cub reporter, had kept away. Suddenly, they had bigger fish to try.

It was, Julia thought, one hell of a price for privacy.

'— *I now place a handful of earth upon his coffin* —'

And now, thanks to Julia's arrogant bluff, another undeserving soul had woken to find her already troubled world ruined forever. They had found Ezra Higgins with his back to an oak, his cloudy eyes staring up through the leaves. In his hand had been a shotgun.

'— *having committed Austin's spirit to eternal rest, we release him to walk hand in hand with the Lord God, Jesus Christ —*'

Julia's fists clenched. By all accounts, Thora Higgins was a simple soul. Born in Broadhurst, she was baptized in this very church, and her father walked her down its aisle eighteen years later to the day. Reading between the *Gazette*'s juicy lines, you'd think she'd never ventured beyond the town's boundaries in her life, and maybe that was true. Her father owned the newsagent's on Bond Street, she went to school here, shopped here, and with the exception of some great-uncle who died in the Crimea, every last one of her ancestors was buried in the same cemetery where Austin was being interred. Where her husband would soon also be buried...

How could Julia have been so stupid? So completely, utterly thoughtless?

Wanted to force Lexie's hand, did you? Well, you made a good job of that, Mrs. McAllister.

Her eyes moved to the weeping stone angels. Far from goading Lexie into making a mistake and giving the police the proof that they needed, Julia's bragging drove her to convince Ezra that the only way out was to take his own life.

'*We will now close up the vault.*'

Austin might rest in peace. Soon Ezra would join him. But dead or alive, Thomas was still out there, and Thomas did not rest in peace. Somehow — God knows how — Julia would make this right.

'*Here ends the ceremony,*' the vicar intoned, '*and a new life begins.*'

'Amen to that,' Julia murmured.

At Chislehurst Hall, Cara pushed back her veil. 'Thank you for coming back with me.'

Julia forced a smile. 'I wouldn't say it's a pleasure exactly, but you know what I mean.'

The Wake was being held at Broadhurst's grandest hotel, in line with Austin's instructions, because even in death, he couldn't resist flaunting his power and wealth. As with all business dealings, though, the invitees were exclusively male, and Julia doubted that even one of them would notice the widow's absence. Or discuss anything other than trade.

'Coffee? Or would you prefer something stronger?'

'Coffee, please, but first, I think my brooch fell off when I was going through Austin's effects.' Lexie didn't have the monopoly on that ploy! 'Mind if I have a look for it?'

Cara shuddered. 'Please excuse me if I don't help, but hell and high water wouldn't drag me back inside that room.'

Exactly what Julia was banking on, because finding Ezra's body had the very opposite effect of what Collingwood wanted. Instead of Blaine investigating Lexie for Austin's murder, the case was now closed. As far as the chief superintendent was concerned, it was irrelevant who may or may not have urged Ezra Higgins to take his own life. Suicide was suicide.

It was over.

As, indeed, was Collingwood's career.

In a bid to bring a kidnapper and killer to justice, he'd left Dudley looking incompetent and made a fool out of Blaine. Proof, as the chief superintendent had insisted all along, that small stations were ineffectual. As of Monday morning, a new detective inspector would be taking over, one whose priority was to integrate the officers, files and prisoners at Boot Street into a larger and more efficient facility. Bang went that ridiculous notion of crime scene photography, too.

Listen carefully, Julia thought. You can hear defeat closing in with every second. Defeat that was entirely her fault, and a man was lying in the mortuary because of it. She didn't regret killing her stepfather, but this? This would haunt her forever, and it didn't matter that Ezra pointed the gun, or that Lexie talked him into pulling the trigger. Julia had handed Lexie the weapon.

But! Defeat isn't the same as surrender, and, unlike bloomer suits, formal dress offered plenty of prospects for concealing bundles of letters. Closing the door to Austin's bedroom behind her, Julia switched on the light and retrieved them from their secret compartment. Alone, they proved nothing, but dammit, even if they were one small cog in establishing Lexie's guilt in both kidnap and murder, and help prove the bitch was still pulling the strings, Collingwood might win a reprieve, Lexie would keep her date with the hangman, and a grieving mother might — just might — find peace.

Checking her reflection in the same mirror that had brought back such traumatic memories of Cara's wedding day, Julia satisfied herself that Lydia's letters were disguised by the clever panelling of her skirts, then cast one final glance round the room.

At the opera glasses focused on the folly. The burr under Austin Forbes' saddle that was both reminder of his failure, but also an incentive to finish the job. At the cheap shepherdess figurine and other second-rate knick-knacks, old ties to his working-class past that had become his spur to success. But, as in all tragedy, there is still humour, if only a glint, and Julia allowed herself a wry smile. Judging by the squiffy angle of the frame, it seemed even the bewigged countess by Joshua

Reynolds disliked the scoundrel who had the temerity to hang her on his bedroom wall. Julia straightened the portrait. Smoothed her jacket. Then turned off the light and rejoined Cara.

'Did you find it?'

'Eventually.' Julia pointed to the little cameo on her blouse. 'Looks like it fell off when I leaned over the dresser.'

Taking a seat on the Louis XV chair, she decided that even the beautiful *cloisonné* work and fine black lacquered Chinese screen couldn't banish the sense of gloom and oppression that hung over Chislehurst Hall. That trudge down the corridor to the Green Room felt more like a walk to the execution chamber, with Austin's censure pulsing out of every Vermeer, and bitterness bouncing off every wall.

No wonder Cara was packing like crazy.

'When DCI Dudley told me they'd found Ezra…' Cara's arm was shaking when she passed Julia the coffee cup. 'I'm sorry, this is going to sound terribly callous, but … the first thought that ran through my head was relief.'

She wasn't alone there, Julia mused. Dudley and Blaine would be throwing their hats in the air, now this political nightmare was behind them.

Or so they believed.

'I was fond of Ezra, you know. When I think of the times I'd cradled his baby… Took the little chap gifts… That's why I didn't believe for one second that he would hurt me. Mind you —' Cara wafted a black ebony fan decorated with sequins and lace — 'I didn't believe him capable of stealing, either. Much less such a large sum! All the same, I'm saddened it ended the way that it did, though I don't understand how he could kill himself without leaving a note.'

'Sadly, only one in four suicides do.'

The majority were too distraught to think beyond death as the solution to their unbearable torment, or a situation from which there was no other escape. Was Ezra one of them? Or had Lexie burned that, as well? But there were a few (luckily only a few), who were too cowardly and too self-obsessed to consider anyone else. A category Henry Davenport fell into with a thud. With any number of meetings with his solicitor when transferring his estate, he could hardly argue that he hadn't had time.

'My marriage was far from perfect, but Austin didn't deserve to die like a dog.'

Cara's lips were pinched white, there were ugly hollows under her eyes, but relief had washed much of the stiffness out of her shoulders, and, in the same way liquor makes weak men bold and cautious men reckless, left an expression of grim determination on Cara's face. Overlaid with what was, still, grief for her husband. Unless...

Unless her grief was for somebody else...

Julia leaned forward. 'I never met him, but I've known men like Austin. Men who mask menace with charm, disguise conceit with good manners, and, because they don't experience guilt, remorse or regret, none of the horror shows itself to the world.'

For proof, look no further than her own stepfather, who had also thrived on power and control drawn from the humiliation of others. Isolation is the bully's secret weapon, and while Julia doubted Austin's torture was physical, it went far beyond his staff walking on eggshells.

He slept with Lexie, knowing the one thing — the only thing — she wanted was to understand why she'd lost everything. Then callously withheld the answer. He knew how hard she'd clawed back from the brink, proving that the Davenports don't back away from a fight, they don't run, they don't hide, and they don't crawl away. Only one Davenport had done that, and Lexie was not like her father. Austin believed he'd broken her, that she'd have to sell up, then, when she didn't, resorted to even dirtier tactics to destroy the Davenport name, taking the only thing Lexie had left. Peace of mind.

Bad blood couldn't run worse.

And then there was Lydia. Out of instinct, anger, repentance, who knows, she returned his letters unopened, and now it was clear why Austin had kept them. Here was one of the few things he couldn't control. He'd continued to bombard her, fully expecting to wear her down with his determination and charm, without realising that she'd been brainwashed into the Davenport mentality. For a man used to getting his own way, Lydia's obstinacy would have rankled. He wrote how he was so choked with emotion that his only communication that day was through sex. *A raw, pulsing, primeval force*, and for a man who never did "anything by halves", Julia had been surprised the walls of the folly were still standing when she first read that note. Then she remembered what he'd written prior to that. *I fear that you believed I was laying claim to you that sunny winter's afternoon. Taking you crudely, as though you were the last piece in my conquest of Lindale Manor.* He went on to say nothing could be further from the truth. In fact, nothing could have been closer. *When I saw that same love reciprocated in those lovely green eyes, I knew I had made a mistake.*

And how! Lydia's account of the affair — two lost, lonely people finding solace in a time of mutual need — was at complete odds with his. In fact, it was pure conceit that made him read love in her eyes. Lydia might not be the last piece in Austin's conquest of Lindale, but it was a crucial one. What he would have seen, if he'd only been able to understand, was shock and revulsion.

This was rape.

After that, she cut off all contact. Seven months later, his baby was kidnapped. And guess where the ransom drop was?

Julia put down her cup, the coffee untouched. 'I know how these things play out, Cara.' Her mother. The slow chipping away of confidence. The constant denigration. The relentless control, bolstering feelings of failure and inadequacy. 'However hard you tried, Austin was never satisfied. The house was never tidy enough. You were never obedient enough. I'm betting your apologies weren't good enough for him, either? Here.' She passed her the second piece of paper that she'd found inside the wallet taped to the underside of the desk. 'No one will ever know about this, except us.'

'When —?' Cara's face turned white. 'Where — did you find this? I searched his pockets, his drawers, I searched everywhere —'

'While searching for my brooch, this was under the bed.'

A masterpiece in humiliation, it might have been written expressly for Julia's mother. Every single aspect of her life had been regimented, from stipulating the precise distance between coat hangers in the wardrobe (three quarters of an inch) to the exact way to fold towels, even the order in which bath salts should be arranged on the shelf.

No wonder Austin kept his vile instructions hidden. Regardless of his wealth and standing, there was a world of difference between a martinet and a sadist. Imagine a valet, a clerk, a secretary stumbling across this. If word got out — and it would only take another "perfidious footman" selling out to the press — how long before his attempts to obliterate the Davenport name came to light? How many other similar tales

197

surfaced in its wake? No businessman worth his salt would back him, befriend him, or be associated with him. *No jam like Forbes* would become no jam at all.

'I … must have lists.' Cara picked at her sleeve. 'With lists, there is order. With order, there is discipline —'

'STOP!' The rage of watching her mother turn into a punchbag welled up in Julia. 'You did nothing wrong. This was his way of cowing you into submission to the point where you couldn't fight back.' Unless it was with a sodding great candlestick beside his coffin. 'You built a wall of defence around yourself that grew into a fortress, but he's gone, and I'd say now's a good time to start knocking the bricks down. To start actually living your life.'

And if Thomas was part of it — dead or alive — Julia, so help her, would move heaven and earth to unite them.

CHAPTER 28

Outside the ironmonger's, the proprietor bustled about, rearranging his bellows and baskets, dishcloths and doorstops, hinges and hammers. The cusp of autumn was also the perfect time to smarten up any peeling paintwork, so he piled cans of varnish and gloss on a trestle table, along with soft bristle brushes in various widths and jars of thinners to tempt passing trade. His diligence might impress Billy Briggs, now a regular at the shop, but it was lost on Julia.

For God's sake, Ezra Higgins' blood wasn't cold and the *Gazette* was seeking fresh stories to fill the front page. "Embezzler kills tycoon, then turns gun on himself" was already old news, and the editor didn't care that a small boy was still missing. An innocent pawn in a deadly feud. His focus was on selling papers and stuffing his pension fund. Right on cue, a horse whinnied, a bicycle bell rang furiously, voices became raised. A confrontation that only needed to escalate a fraction — an extra insult, a punch — and that same editor could run with his favourite theme: the record number of bicycles on the road, and what a threat they were to society. Since cycling crossed every social divide, provoking arguments about the emancipation of women guaranteed to have papers flying off the press. How could an old, unsolved kidnap compete with debates about bloomers?

Threading through the maze of the Saturday market, its stalls spilling over with pears and plums, chickens and ducks, and churns of bright yellow butter, Julia understood why the shopkeepers of Broadhurst sported cleaner aprons, smarter armbands, and stiffer collars than their counterparts here in Oakbourne, and why they swaggered around in brand new straw hats. It was the same reason Cara hadn't moved a muscle throughout the entire funeral service or the subsequent committal. The same reason Julia maintained the lie that Sam Whitmore was still alive and running the studio. The same reason Lexie wore blue buttoned boots that could have paid for a new floor, and why she created exquisite botanical gardens.

Image.

But since image was most killers' weak point, and it was certainly Lexie's, it was also the best point of attack.

Yet even as a plan began to form, Julia couldn't rid herself of the feeling that she'd missed something in Austin's room. She patted the bundle inside her skirts. Not them. In fact, she'd scanned the whole place before switching the light off, and nothing struck her as odd. And yet...

'Good God, Billy Briggs, how long have I been gone?'

The grass inspector stepped back to admire his handiwork. 'Coming along nice, innit?'

'You've transformed the whole studio!' In the space of two days, this was back to being an establishment "the nobs round here" *would* be happy to be seen entering. 'I honestly can't thank you enough.'

Oh, Sam. If you could see it now!

'Why? You bought the varnish, all I done was slap it on, and that's the thing when you got nimble fingers like me. Used to working fast with me brasses.'

'There's only one word I can think of that rhymes with that.'

Billy chuckled. 'Only 'cause you got a dirty mind. Brass bands, luv.' He waggled them. 'Hands.'

'And you still found time to pull on the eyepatch and hang around stations.'

'As long as I'm 'ere, I won't stop looking out for them kids, and besides, I've seen what happens when tramps have got nuffin' to do. They end up drinking methylated spirits and dying a slow, 'orrible death, but the way I see it, turps gives yer burps, best keep moving.'

Can't make friends if you don't put down roots, he said once. Isn't that an equally slow, 'orrible death?

'Anyways.' He tilted his head at the china mastiff on the top shelf in the window. 'Be a relief to get away from that ugly brute, 'cause swear to God, wherever I'm standing, whatever angle I'm bent at, it's watchin' me.'

'The sign of true art, Billy. The best portraits are those where the eyes follow you round the room.' (Yes, Bewigged Countess, I mean you!)

'Nah. Them portraits of yours? The weddings, the christenings, the family gatherings? They're more than just photographs, luv. You caught their characters in them frames, and that, my girl, is true art.'

Julia put the kettle on, brought out a bag of soft, crumbly lemon biscuits and set them on a plate. 'The second the shutter on my camera opens, I'm very much aware that I'm capturing a unique moment in that person's life. And since it's frozen for all time, it's only right that it should reflect their personality and emotions, in fact the whole essence of their being. Otherwise, what's the point?'

Take that banker last week. His employers wouldn't allow him to have a personal portrait taken on work premises, so at Julia's suggestion, a team of men lugged his desk to her studio and they recreated his office here, instead. Right down to his buttoned swivel chair, inkwell, pens, cigar clipper and snuff box!

'Told yer before how you don't think like everybody else. Take them farm scenes of yours. Who else'd lay five photos on top of one another to end up with what looks like a simple snap of the moment?' Billy scratched his stubble. 'Then again, I never imagined you'd have to strap babies in some contraption the Spanish Inquisition would be proud of, just to stop the little bleeders wrigglin' about.'

'It's called a baby positioning stand,' she said, dunking her lemon biscuit in her coffee, 'and —'

Wait. Inkwell? Pens? Cigar clipper? Snuff box? All the way home, Julia couldn't put her finger on what niggled about Austin's bedroom, now it clicked.

The valuables in his display case were gone.

'Gone?'

Julia pictured Cara at the other end of the telephone, sinking down on the crushed-velvet sofa. Any colour left in her face would be drained, as the burden of horrors was now compounded by the knowledge that someone had broken into her home, sifted through personal belongings.

'Take a look for yourself, you'll see —'

'No! I'm never going back in that room!' There was a pause, while Cara composed herself. 'The display case, you say?'

'I could be wrong about exactly which items are missing —' this is where Lydia's razor-sharp memory would come in useful — 'but I do know the tortoiseshell snuff box has gone, along with a pair of gold cufflinks. You need to call the police.'

'I appreciate your concern, my dear, but I've already had to sack one footman for his perfidious betrayal —'

'I don't think it's an inside job, Cara.'

Why risk it, when the mistress was leaving, and they'd have the luxury to pick items with a much higher value over a long period of time? A cat burglar, on the other hand, working with a small matchless flashlight, needed saleable objects that slipped into a pocket, and this little haul followed the pattern of stealing items that didn't instantly stand out.

I don't know about you, but I'd say one of the softest targets is the house the police move away from, Lexie had said.

She was right. Except Lindale Manor wasn't the target, and, as Julia hung the receiver back in its cradle, she wondered how many times the cat had dipped into that particular pot of cream? Because if the jewel thief was familiar with Chislehurst Hall, what else might they know without realising its importance?

Catch the cat, she thought, and they might just trap the mouse.

CHAPTER 29

'This leaves me somewhat conflicted.' Collingwood thumbed through the scene of crime photos in Julia's studio. 'Do I clap him on the back, or do I clap him in irons?'

'The one good thing about this robbery is that it's a professional job.'

That the thief had been watching the property was obvious. He pounced the instant police presence decreased and the press had decamped.

'Half of me hopes you're wrong about this.' Collingwood grimaced at the photograph of the pool of blood where Austin staunched the wound with his necktie. 'With their ability to sneak in and out without making a sound, stealing jewels from the rich, cat burglars enjoy hero status among the lower classes.' He snorted. 'Wonder how they'd feel if the boot was on the other foot, and someone stole a ring that had belonged to *their* mother, the only reminder of her that they had?' For thieves, a rare first edition spells cash, he added, not a gift from a beloved son, just as a chess set dating back four hundred years is seen in terms of monetary, not historical, value. 'Makes me sick to my stomach, merely thinking about making a deal with this scum, but, as much as it galls me, cat burglars know where to strike, which means they've spent a lot of time walking the floors, noting the treasures and assessing their value.'

Julia tried not to think how she'd feel, knowing strangers had been in her room while she slept, going through her clothes and fingering her underwear.

'Small items, like the cufflinks and snuff box,' he said, 'he's unlikely to trail all the way to London to fence. But at the same time, he won't want to offload them on his own doorstep.' For the first time in a long time, Collingwood looked like the man Julia recognised. The tracker who never lets up. 'And since his haul is fresh and we know what pieces we're looking for, I'll have my men lean on our local dealers. See if we can't pick him up quickly.'

Outside, clouds had swirled in, heavy and low.

'What if I'm wrong?'

'Then at least I leave Boot Street knowing people can sleep soundly in their beds at night.' A wry smile twisted his face. 'I owe you one, Mrs. McAllister.'

She swallowed. Little did he know it was the other way round. Julia intended to keep it that way.

Yes, he knew she was hiding behind a false identity, and yes, he'd given his word to stop probing. But when you kill a man and it's premeditated murder, regardless of the circumstances, you hang. Thanks to his promise, the shadow of the noose had receded. Receded, but not gone away.

Collingwood was relentless, ambitious, dedicated to justice and the truth. Once his grief had tempered and his anger assuaged, he'd have nothing left but his job. And his job was bringing killers to justice.

As the wind howled through the trees, Julia realised that his being sacked was the one thing that would save her. And, in that instant, she saw a way to find Thomas, trap Lexie, and still put her dark past behind her.

Could she do it? She glanced at him, leafing through the records of the murder scene. Would she really stab him in the back, when he was at rock bottom? If she had the funds, she'd change her name and disappear without trace. Unfortunately, thanks to that last nasty business, she'd given everything away

— one crisis at a time and all that. Suddenly, though, here was her chance to seal the past once and for all.

Only a fool would turn that opportunity down.

'Actually, Inspector, I think you'll find you owe me quite a few,' Julia quipped, but the taste in her mouth was bitter and vile. As the taste of betrayal should be.

'There's one suspect Blaine didn't consider, when he was heading the investigation into Thomas' disappearance.' Collingwood started to pace. 'Grace Davenport.'

'For God's sake, she was a child!'

'Exactly. Intent on punishing the man she blamed for her grandfather's death, she'd only have meant to scare Austin by snatching his son, and if she's young for her age now, imagine her at ten, when she wasn't — indeed still isn't — used to handling children.'

'You think Grace accidentally smothered the boy?'

'Suggesting would be a better word, but it explains why her mother would cover it up. The only drawback in that theory is that I can't see Ezra going along with it later, no matter how hard Lexie leaned on him.'

'Try this for size.' Julia stopped trying to follow Collingwood's pacing. It put caged tigers to shame and was making her dizzy. 'For fifteen years, Austin and Cara have no physical contact, then out of nowhere she gives birth to a son. Remember how the first two Forbes babies were weak? One didn't live through her first day, the other didn't survive her first week. Thomas, on the other hand, was a sturdy little ox. Now maybe that's because...'

'He came from hardier stock.'

Julia thought of Cara's grief-stricken face. The photo in the *Gazette* of a small boy with a froth of curls. And parents who both had straight hair. 'A wife abandoned in all but name. A book-keeper who spends his working life shut away from the world. Why shouldn't two lonely people find solace together? Also,' she added slowly, 'it fits with the theory that the two crimes are connected.'

From the outset, Ezra would have known he was the father, just as he knew that, at some point, a cuckoo's feathers will start to stand out.

'Fearing Austin's reaction, or perhaps simply wanting to protect his child, he abducted the boy, and since he couldn't raise him alone, certainly not in Broadhurst, maybe he found a family to take him?'

'Then why kill Austin eight years later?'

'Did I say my theory was perfect?'

'Most likely Cara admitted her affair —'

'Trust me, Inspector, that woman would tear out her heart, lungs and liver with her bare hands before admitting Thomas was a bastard conceived through adultery.'

'Neither does it explain Lexie's involvement, because hers isn't the behaviour of an innocent woman.' Collingwood stopped pacing. 'Actually, I didn't drop by to talk about cat burglars and toss out theories that get wilder by the minute.' He laid the crime scene photos face down on the table, his expression as black as the sky. 'Have you seen this?'

From his pocket he pulled out the front page of the *Broadhurst Gazette*.

MURDERED BY HIS MOTHER!

Long after Collingwood left, Julia continued to stare at the headlines. Credit where it was due, the reporter had done a thorough job of piecing together Thora Higgins' pain. How the man she'd loved — apparently worshipped wasn't too strong a word — turned out to be a stranger to her. A murderer, a thief, a liar and a coward, whose cottage door was now pelted regularly with rotten fruit (and worse). Between the charlady and the woman who took in their washing, it seemed Thora was more than capable of coping with the fish-eye stares, at being hissed and spat at, and the lies about how she was complicit from the start, had already spent half the money that he'd stolen, even handed him the shotgun on that fateful morning.

What she couldn't take was the effect it would have on her son. All his life, he'd be pointed at, bullied, taunted because bad blood ran in his veins. No one would befriend a monster, consequently, her son would never find a decent job, or take a wife and raise a family of his own, for the simple reason that no one would see the goodness in him.

With nowhere to hide, nowhere to run, and no way to escape her husband's betrayal, Thora took the only sensible course of action. She held a pillow over her baby's face, then filled the bathtub and opened her wrists.

Child killers sell papers, so the *Gazette* called it murder. Thora, of course, called it mercy. Julia called it tragedy out of all proportion. Her only hope was that Cara was too busy packing to reach for the news, or to read how Thora dressed the boy in his christening robes before smothering him.

CHAPTER 30

Throughout the towns and countryside, church bells pealed in the ever-optimistic hope that sinners would see the errors of their ways and spend their Sunday mornings repenting. Unfortunately, factory workers preferred the public house to God's, while families gathered round the Sunday roast in their finery. Either way, though, Sundays were designed for exchanging news, inventing gossip, borrowing money, and talking about people behind their backs, not prayer. The time when jealousies surfaced, rifts were healed, made or deepened, and grandchildren spoiled rotten. God could be found in all these things, the sinners argued. We'll spend enough time with Him when we're dead.

Julia watched the rain hammering against the glass and making lakes in the street. Death was all she could think of. Her father. Her stepfather. Sam Whitmore. Henry Davenport. Austin Forbes. Ezra Higgins. Now Thora Higgins. Cradling a glass of cognac between her hands, unable to drink it but unable to sleep, she'd spent the night in her darkroom — her one place of refuge — reflecting on the toll this feud had taken. On how too many people had been snared in its web. And how, as always, the innocents suffered.

Below her window, children squealed as they jumped in the puddles. Angry parents pulled them away. What Ezra's parents would give, to see their grandson soaked to the skin! How cross would Cara be, if that was Thomas?

Julia pictured her, frantically filling her trunks with beaver hats and sealskin capes, fur, of course, not permitted during mourning. Not that her maid was incapable of packing the right things. It was simply that the hands of the clock pass considerably faster when you're sorting fans, gloves and parasols yourself, and this wouldn't be the first chink in the armour of standards that needed to be upheld at all times. Cara, it seemed, wasn't the only person who hadn't gone into Austin's bedroom. After straightening the picture frame then patting down her skirts to be sure the letters didn't show, her thumb left a mucky mark on the material that still wouldn't wash out. A far cry from the spotless, gleaming frames that lined the corridor to the Green Room. And if that was just a couple of days, God knows what was going to slip, once Cara packed up, because without Austin, who would drum into the servants that status must, repeat *must*, be maintained. That appearances must not be allowed to slip. Not once, and not ever.

Julia imagined Cara running through the same old mantra, about how the key to survival was keeping control, just as the key to keeping control was discipline and routine.

Regardless of who had broken into her house and who hadn't.

Her thoughts turned from Chislehurst Hall to Lindale Manor, and the sherry Lexie served on the terrace, forty years in the barrel.

A long time in the planning…

Revamping the gardens three weeks after her father's funeral was far from coincidence, neither was Lexie's dismissal of the "small army" of gardeners and servants, which dovetailed with Dickon's arrival. When Thomas disappeared, the police searched the Manor and grounds with a fine tooth comb, and if Blaine came up empty, Julia was damn sure it's because there was nothing to find. What odds that blood, fish and bone fertiliser threw the dogs off the scent he had blazed? Or those same sharp noses had been thwarted by mud and pondweed, after the ornamental lake had been dredged? He couldn't dig up every square inch on a hunch, Blaine had told Collingwood. The Davenports were too well-respected in Broadhurst. His superiors just wouldn't sanction it.

The bitch got away with it, Collingwood had told Julia bitterly, adding that it's a sad fact of life that not all killers are caught. Only those who weren't smart enough to destroy every trace.

Very well, then! Julia reached for her hat. With time running out and the physical evidence gone, there was only one thing left.

'Just so yer know.' Billy draped his dripping jacket over the back of the kitchen chair and hung his frayed cap on the stand. 'I'll be leavin' tomorrer.'

Julia should have guessed. Friendship was quicksand when you're outrunning heartbreak: once you're in, it's hard to get out. She should know. 'I haven't thanked you properly for the work you've done. Stay at least until Wednesday.' *Thursday. Please…*

'Hey, yer've fed me till me buttons burst, that's thanks enough, and besides, it ain't like the work's finished. Them frames still need another weasel.'

'Easel? Teasel? Give me a clue.'

'Weasel and stoat.' He chuckled. 'Coat. Talking of which, you off to confession?'

'In a manner of speaking. I'm headed for Lindale Manor.'

'Then suppose I walk yer to the bus? I hold the brolly, you got both hands free to keep that pretty skirt of yours out the puddles. As a special bonus, I get to punch any driver what deliberately tries to soak yer.'

Billy didn't look like he could punch a paper bag, but Julia appreciated the thought. 'Certainly not. You're a drowned rat as it is.'

'Skin don't shrink, luv, and y'know the best bit? Damn stuff's waterproof. Come on!'

'Honestly, it's fine, I'm taking a cab. There's usually one at the stand on the corner.'

'In that case, I'll go take a look-see.'

Julia was catching on to this Cockney rhyming slang lark. Look-see. Pee. 'Second door on the left.'

'No.' For a very short word, he managed to drag out four syllables. 'I'll. Go. Take. A. Look… Whistle him over…'

As the rain drummed against the sides of the cab, Julia's eyes stung. 'Why don't you stay?' she had asked. 'Take a chance that the grass on the other side might actually be the same colour?'

'And do what?' he'd snorted. 'No one's gonna give a tramp like me a job, and you've seen 'em, rushing the factory gates when they open, hoping for work. I'm the last one they'd pick, and me hands is too rough to go back to gloves.'

'But the banter, the companionship, someone to share meals with. Won't you miss that?'

Sam, Sam, it's been nearly five years. Why does it still hurt like hell?

As the cab clopped down Cadogan Street, she knew she would have to make a decision.

Either accept the emptiness that came from being Julia McAllister, in which case, she'd need to revive the dirty picture sideline pretty damn quick to keep the studio running and fund her independence.

Or follow the examples of Billy and Cara. Go as far, and as fast, as she could. Make a clean start, with a new identity, where friends wouldn't be kept at arm's length.

Wiping away the hot tears of shame — there were never any winners in domestic abuse — Julia forced her thoughts back to the reason she was in this cab in the first place.

Ezra Higgins was known to have been conscientious, hard-working, financially sound, respected by shopkeepers, colleagues and neighbours, in fact no one had a bad word to say about him.

On the other hand, Austin Forbes' reputation was nowhere near as shining. A tyrant at home, a bully at work, a serial adulterer into the bargain, many people believed he got what he deserved.

But does anyone deserve both barrels of a shotgun at close range?

Julia lifted her eyes to the towering factories and chimneys. To the filth being washed down by the rain. Even a bastard isn't all bad, and ultimately only Austin Forbes knew what made him who — and what — he was. The pressures of rising from a working-class background to millionaire manufacturer of jam production that secured a Royal Warrant could not be underestimated. In an exhausting, exacting and competitive industry, where harvests fail from maggots in the apple trees to aphids, slugs and weevils in the cane fruit, but demand remains higher than ever, it was a constant battle of expand-or-fail. In business you cannot stand still.

Then there was the question of Austin's heir. Julia remembered reading a piece in the basement archive of the *Broadhurst Gazette* about Austin's brother who was killed in 1885 fighting the Mad Mahdi in a bid to save Khartoum. With a wife who had no head for business, two daughters who'd died in the first stages of infancy, and his son abducted and never heard of again, who would take over his hard-won legacy?

Character is formed under pressures like this. They make weak men crumble, and turn hard men into despots. In that respect, she supposed, Forbes was no different from anyone else, and it didn't hurt that his uncompromising reputation preceded him. One has to be hard-nosed in business.

Firm? Yes. But was he fair?

Stubborn sod, too. Never overturned a decision in his life.

Was that such a bad thing? If he'd been wronged — like his book-keeper, stealing a whopping three hundred pounds, or a bunch of feckless workers who faced him down on Christmas Eve — his actions were swift and decisive.

Even so, contradictions abounded. Austin despised weakness and didn't suffer fools gladly, and nowhere was that clearer than his contempt for Henry Davenport, in not facing up to his obligations. But wouldn't a despot brag about taking his land? Austin remained tight-lipped from beginning to end, and the same applied to the incident on Christmas Eve. The timing was poor, as the head gardener had said, but his workers picked the fight, not him. They just chose the wrong man to pick it with. Yet who paid the hospital bill?

Screwed creditors and women in equal measure, said the grocer off-loading flour sacks from the cart in the alley. But did he? It would only take one disgruntled creditor to air a grudge before others jumped on the bandwagon, and figures don't lie. The police had examined Austin's accounts in meticulous detail, where it soon became clear that if someone was in genuine difficulty, he extended the deadline for repayment, in some cases more than once. Which took Julia back to the question of who actually accused him of screwing his creditors? The ones who owed him money then jibbed about paying, of course. Rich swell, he could afford to write it off, they'd argue. Never mind the hours Austin worked to bring about that success, the slog he put in to secure that "lucky" Royal seal of appointment, or the bugger-all they contributed their end.

Wait —!

1885. Austin's brother died in 1885.

Thomas was born in 1886.

Tyrant, bully, serial adulterer or not, the death of his brother, the only tie to his bloodline, in a battle that lasted a mere fifteen minutes and still failed to save Khartoum, would make any man take stock of his life. More than ever, Austin would want — need — an heir, or everything he'd achieved would be in vain.

Did he win Cara over with the charm he famously turned on and off?

Did he take her by force, like he took Lydia at the folly?

Did it matter? When his son was kidnapped, Austin had none of the usual outlets for grief. Even his wife had escaped to Provence, leaving him to drown his misery in the time-honoured tradition of wine, women and song.

As the cab pulled up outside Lindale Manor, the anomalies gnawed like sharp little rats' teeth.

Time, Julia decided, to call the Pied Piper.

CHAPTER 31

'Quick, quick, quick! Come in, out of this horrible weather!'

With her upswept hair, not a strand out of place, not a crinkle in her skirt, Lydia would have fitted right in among the satins and silks bustling in and out of the *parfumiers* of Paris, sweeping down the *Champs Elysées*, or drinking champagne by the Seine. Julia could just picture the honeymoon couple, top hats raised in admiration wherever they went, paying tribute to both Lydia's elegance and Henry Davenport's luck. Even now, with paint splashes over her dress, her arms, her hands, her nose, Lydia would still turn heads.

'What do you know about Joshua Reynolds?' Julia asked

Lydia stumbled. Or perhaps slipped from where Julia shook the drips off her hem. 'He painted portraits. Died over a hundred years ago. Why do you ask?'

'Austin hung a countess on his bedroom wall.' Julia paused. 'It reminded me of you.'

'Lexie and Grace should be back from church shortly. Not that they're fervent, it's just that —'

'I know. The Davenports need to keep up appearances.' Julia followed her into the drawing room. 'I'm glad it's just us, because I wanted to give you these.'

'Austin's letters?'

Despite her hopes, they shed no light on either the kidnap or the murder, and since Julia was certain Lydia had played no part in either, there was only one person who should have them. The addressee. 'He loved you, Lydia.'

Love is not the preserve of the young.
Love is what lives in our hearts.

216

Lines penned by a middle-aged man to a beautiful, much younger woman, these were hardly the slick lines of the shallow adulterer, or a man trying to claw back time.

'And I loved him.' Lydia sank down on the sofa with characteristic grace. 'Just not the same way he felt about me.' She loved *loving* him, if that made any sense. It made her feel alive, made her feel beautiful, but most of all, she said, it made her feel wanted. 'At first, the affair was nothing more than my way of getting back at Henry for not being around, and putting cards and dice above me. But within two months I'd learned more about history, geography, travel and music than I had in my entire life. I couldn't give him up if I tried.'

'Why didn't you tell Lexie about Henry's gambling addiction?'

'What was the point? She'd only have accused me of making it up, of trying to drive a wedge between her and her father.' Lydia hugged the letters to her chest. 'When I heard that Austin had died, I thought it would be the closing of a chapter. Instead, I find myself missing him so badly, it's like a knife through my heart, and there's guilt, as well, because I never saw my husband's face in the sunset, or heard my husband's voice in the wind the way I did with Austin, and I will go to my grave regretting returning these letters unopened.' Rainwater pounded the roof tiles, and gurgled down the lead gutter pipes. 'Since he died,' she continued, 'and this will sound foolish, but I've spent far too much time at that folly than is good for me.'

'Hardly foolish. Men like Austin leave a powerful presence behind.'

'Thank you, dear.' Lydia reached out and squeezed Julia's hand, leaving a blob of blue paint on her wrist. 'The first time, I expected my conscience to haunt me. A reminder of lands re-assigned. Of unsatisfactory marriages. Of the things that had gone wrong with both of our lives. Instead, I felt lighter, if you can understand. Don't get me wrong, the pain of loss hasn't diminished, but…'

'It was like a weight had been lifted?'

'Exactly! And as I relived the — excuse my vulgarity, but the animal passion of our last meeting, I truly felt Austin's forgiveness.'

Julia wanted to say there was nothing to forgive. Austin was married, and *that* was his regret. She wanted to tell her about the opera glasses trained on the folly, reminding him of what was quite possibly the only time in his life when he'd been happy. Voices in the hall put paid to that.

'How insulting, Mama!' Grace's anger probably rattled the roof tiles. 'How utterly demeaning! In this day and age, how can it be acceptable for a woman to take a job as a postmistress, a shop girl, a waitress, a cook, but unacceptable for a woman to take up a proper career?' Her mother's voice remained calm and was therefore muffled. 'I'm going to join the suffrage movement, Mama, you can't stop me, and you wait. By the time you're old and grey, women like me will have changed the world!'

Though Lexie's muffle grew louder, Julia only caught the part about 'you're not a woman' before Lydia ran to the rescue, threatening to throw a bucket of water over both of them, if they didn't stop. A clumping of boots and the slamming of a door testified to what Grace thought about that.

'Leave her, darling,' Lydia told her stepdaughter. Behind them, a young man with gypsy curls melted away. 'You put your feet up, I'll go and calm her down.'

'Aaarrgh!' Lexie threw herself onto the sofa and reached for a button hook. 'I swear a dozen grey hairs appear every time I see that girl.' She heaved off the first finely tooled white leather boot. 'Independence this, independence that, all because she read about some silly movement in America where women choose to remain single, live alone, and manage their own careers and affairs.'

'Bachelor maids,' Julia said.

'You've heard of them?'

Off came the second boot, and Julia calculated how that pair alone could have re-laid the floor where her kitten heels had a fight with the woodworm. 'So have you, Lexie. Look in the mirror.'

'Fair point. Good to see you again, by the way! I hope you've brought good news with you this time, I could certainly use a large dose.'

'Sorry to disappoint you.'

'Then I'd better find another way to erase that tedious sermon and that even more tedious daughter of mine.' She padded across to the sideboard in her stockinged feet, opened the oloroso and poured two generous glasses. *A long time in the planning...* 'Come on, then.' Lexie massaged her bunions. 'Let's get the hard part over and done with.'

Julia sipped. Whether for keeping up appearances or not, this sherry, like Lexie, was truly exquisite. 'From the outset,' she said, 'I knew Thomas's kidnap and Austin's murder were connected.'

'A tragedy further compounded when poor Thora killed her baby and herself, because she couldn't see any other way forward.'

'Tragedy being the right word, because her husband, unfortunately, did not.'

'Didn't what?'

'I'll show you.' Julia left the room, returning in less than a minute with a length of timber used for repairs. 'Imagine your wall is an oak tree and this piece of wood is my shotgun.' She positioned herself on the floor, with her back to the wall, the same way Collingwood had in her studio yesterday, using one of her props as the gun.

Because that was the real purpose behind his dropping by yesterday. Not to exchange theories. Not to show her the newspaper article about Thora Higgins. Collingwood had called to talk about Ezra.

'This walking cane is roughly the right length,' he'd told Julia, grabbing one of the studio props. 'Making the trigger right about here.'

'Quite a stretch.'

'Now imagine Ezra, a good five, six inches shorter than me, trying to reach it.'

Carefully, Julia re-enacted the piece. Ten seconds passed. Twenty. Then Lexie was Lexie again. 'He could have gripped the shotgun between his feet,' she said levelly, 'then pulled the trigger using some kind of tool. A long stick, perhaps? He was in the woods, after all.'

'That wouldn't explain how the gun was found in his hand, when the blast went straight through his heart.'

The silence between them stretched to infinity. The wind howled out Julia's pain.

'My father managed perfectly well.'

Julia let the timber drop. 'Lexie, your father planned his suicide to the very last detail. He secured the shotgun to the leg of his desk, thus making one hundred per cent certain that it wouldn't recoil, and therefore wouldn't miss. Then he tied a piece of string to the trigger and pulled.'

'Wh-what are you saying? The same person who shot Austin also k-killed Ezra?'

'I don't think, Lexie. I know. Do you want to know their mistake?'

'Killing Ezra?'

'Being too squeamish to blow his head off.'

Lexie perched on the sofa, clutching a cushion to stop her hands shaking.

'You have no proof.'

'Damn right.' The hands on the clock seemed to have been glued into place. 'What I need is a confession.'

'You won't get one.'

Lexie knew it. Julia knew it. But —

'I know what you've done, Lexie, and I know why you did it —'

'Then you know I did it for the right reasons.'

'— but dragging Dickon, Lydia, even your own daughter, into your web can't *ever* be justified. Have you stopped to think what will happen to them in prison?'

Lexie jumped to her feet. 'The Davenports don't run from a fight, and they never back down! When push comes to shove, we fight back, and more importantly we fight hard.'

'Interesting that you didn't mention anything about fighting fair.'

'I will always do what I have to do, Julia, however distasteful, but you must understand. Grace, Lydia, Dickon? They're just pawns in this. For pity's sake, can't you keep them out of it?'

'No.'

'Please! I am begging you!'

'This isn't about you, or me, it's about evidence, Lexie. But —' Sickness churned in Julia's stomach. Suddenly, the wood at her feet was no longer a prop. This was the shotgun that Henry used to take his own life. The same shotgun that also killed Ezra. '— there is another way out.'

CHAPTER 32

'I do apologise for turning up unannounced, Cara.'

'Nonsense, Julia! You have no idea how glad I am to see a friendly face! Come. Let's retire to the Green Room. We can talk without long ears twitching, because if that horrible burglary wasn't enough, I read that Thora killed her baby then committed suicide. Dear God, the waste of it all! The tragedy of it all! Where is it going to end?'

Julia watched the raindrops race one another down the glass, thinking how the weather made this depressing mould-green room more gloomy than Hades, and not a fraction as cheerful. 'Actually, Cara, that's the reason I'm here,' she said. 'I think you'd better sit down.'

She turned her gaze from the window to the woman with the tiny waist and enormous puff sleeves, and exquisite dress with the black velvet bolero. Cara was still rigid, still pale, still exhausted from lack of sleep. But already there were signs that a new era was beginning. A sense of what freedom would bring.

More than anything, Julia had wanted to give this woman answers.

The answers she had would not bring Cara peace.

'The past eight years have been very difficult for you,' Julia said. 'The strain, the tension, the fear.'

Cara swallowed. 'You have no idea.'

'Actually I do.' Julia drew a deep breath. 'You see, I've talked to a police officer friend of mine, an inspector, and he's pretty sure he knows what happened that night.'

'Thomas?' Cara clamped a trembling hand over her mouth. 'Don't tell me they've found him!'

'No.' Oh, God, this was awful. Julia needed to handle it better than this. 'Let's start with Ezra.'

'They're saying he kidnapped my son.' Cara rubbed her temple. 'But I don't understand. Why would Ezra kidnap my son?'

'He didn't. Just as he was set up to take the fall for your husband's murder.'

'But he admitted stealing the three hundred pounds! It was even found in his sideboard.'

'The police aren't saying he didn't steal the money. What they're saying is, he didn't kidnap your son.' Julia took a deep heaving breath. 'And he didn't kill Austin, either.' She perched on the edge of the Louis XV chair, every bit as uncomfortable as she remembered. 'After Thomas was abducted —' Careful, careful. Ease her in gently. This was going to knock the stuffing right out of her — 'the police, as you know, focused their enquiries on Lexie Davenport.'

'I knew she had an axe to grind, accusing Austin of stealing her inheritance, and I knew she was familiar with the layout of this house. I just couldn't believe another mother would stoop so low as to kidnap a child.'

'Driven women are a force to be reckoned with, and Lexie was certainly bitter. But her anger was directed at her father for selling out his family then cowardly killing himself. She had no motive to shoot Austin.'

'Who, then —? Oh, my God! I knew he and Lydia were at it like rabbits, but as the years passed, believe me when I say I gave up caring who my husband was bedding, providing he was discreet.' Cara sighed. 'What happened? There's no need to wrap it up, Julia. Did he discard her, like he did everyone else? Hell hath no fury I know, but my God! If she wanted to get back at Austin, why punish my angel boy?'

Julia clasped her hands together. This was one of the hardest things she'd ever done. Behind them, the rain hammered the glass. 'Lydia didn't take your son, either.'

Cara had to brace herself for the truth. To face the nightmare head on.

'So — if it wasn't Lexie, and it wasn't Lydia … oh!' Cara clamped both hands to her mouth. 'Oh, dear God. *Austin.* That's why my baby didn't cry out! But why? Why, Julia? His own son! Did he think the boy was another man's child? Just because Thomas was healthy and strong? But yes, it makes sense. Locking me indoors after the kidnap. Convincing me it was to protect me from the press, while he set up the ransom and dealt with the kidnappers — oh, God, he had it all planned, didn't he! This way, he still keeps the money, but … but punishes me in the cruellest way possible!'

'Kidnap's an effective smokescreen,' Julia rasped, 'and it explains why the ransom wasn't touched. Except Austin didn't take Thomas from his cot, Cara.' She leaned forward. 'You did.'

CHAPTER 33

'I had no choice.' Cara buried her head in her hands. 'Believe me, I felt sick to my heart that so many good, honest people were giving up so much of their time, but for my baby's sake — for his safety — I had to keep quiet, and if I went to jail for the rest of my life, I swear on my baby's eyes, every second behind bars would be worth it. Safe in the knowledge that he'd never be beaten, because you were right when you said nothing was ever good enough for Austin. Nothing could ever be right.' The look she shot Julia was of unadulterated pain. 'If there was one thing I learned over the years, it was how to hide the hurt that he caused, and when Thomas was born I vowed, then and there, that Austin wouldn't have the chance to mould my son in his own vile image, or bully him until he ended up cowed and browbeaten like me.'

Julia thought of the servants, gliding like ghosts, their faces turned to the floor. The terrible, terrible silence. 'So you set up the kidnap and arranged the adoption. The wrong thing for the right reasons?'

Cara slumped back in her chair. 'You have no idea what it's like to be able to talk about it after all these years. The relief!' She closed her eyes. 'I promised my baby, as I lifted him from his cot, that he would never have to cower at the sound of his father's footsteps.' Her voice was little more than a whisper. 'That from then on, he'd only know love.'

Julia could not bear to meet Cara's eye. She took a deep breath and let it out slowly. 'Do you ever see him? Thomas?'

'I can't.' Cara swallowed. 'I daren't.'

'No. Of course not.' Julia thought of the shattered photograph frame on the floor. The last photo taken of

225

Thomas. 'No judge will send you to prison for the rest of your life, Cara. Even though you misled the police, I can promise, you won't rot in jail.'

The change was instant. Cara's spine slackened. The tension in her jaw fell away. Suddenly Cara looked five — ten — years younger. A stunningly beautiful, radiant woman. One for whom sleep would finally come.

'Oh, Julia. I'm so glad Fate brought us together outside the hat shop.' Her eyes shone with tears. 'You have no idea what this means to me.'

'I do. Believe me I do.' Julia leaned forward. 'What it means for you, Cara, is the noose.'

Lies. Nothing but lies and deception from beginning to end. The magician's art of misdirection executed to perfection, by a woman who acted Sarah Bernhardt right off the stage.

A tyrant at home, a despot at work, a serial adulterer and quite possibly wife-beater into the bargain? Everything pointed to the same picture of Austin, but the deeper Julia thought about it, the more contradictory the evidence. A man who carried forward not just one, but several debts for two, sometimes three years, didn't tally with a man with "a broad network of enemies". More someone who knew how tough survival could be in these industrialised times, but whose reputation was smeared by jealous competitors and embittered ex-workers.

The haberdashery assistant was adamant that Mrs. Forbes was never, and she meant never, late. Of course, being punctual for appointments didn't mean much in itself. Nor, come to that, did a desire to be left alone by the press. Except this didn't tie up with such a private individual spilling her guts to her milliner. Unless she wanted gossip spread all over town…

Cara dripped her poison with care. A veiled allegation here, a whispered hint there. Nothing substantial, where the finger could be pointed. No, no, Cara was refined, Cara was a martyr, she held herself with dignity and didn't complain.

As a result, everyone but everyone admired and felt sorry for her. *Cara Forbes has been to hell and back*, Dudley said. By keeping the press at arm's length, she'd contrived to outwit them, because all the while, it was Austin who was the victim of domestic abuse. He was the one who'd been given the notebook, specifying how far apart coat hangers should be set, how to arrange the bath salts, in which order. So ashamed of his secret that he kept it locked away, in case his manservant should stumble across it, just like the last remaining photograph of his son. Hidden, so no one but he would see Thomas — certainly not the wife, who'd crushed his spirit and emasculated him, and would take even that last memory from him, if she could.

That's why Cara stormed out of the room. Furious that he'd disobeyed her and there was no way to punish him, the same fury that made her destroy the chapel. And the hell she needed Julia's help to search his personal effects for compromising correspondence. The bitch needed a character witness — and that look of triumph she recalled in the mirror? That was on Cara's face. Not on Austin's.

'For eight years your husband threw everything into finding Thomas, and probably never gave up hoping he was alive. What happened? I can't believe he stumbled across a nine-year-old in Kensington and thought, *I'll bet that's my long-lost son.*'

'Of course not. Even I didn't know where Thomas had gone. Moving out of the area was a condition of sale —' Cara stopped. Too late to change *sale* to *adoption*. 'Don't look at me like that!' Even cornered, Cara Forbes oozed refinement and style. 'With no money of my own, why shouldn't I be recompensed for giving up my precious, long-awaited angel?'

'You can dispense with the angel bollocks, too. You killed your daughters, didn't you?'

'Babies aren't people, Julia. They have no character of their own, no personality, they're simply smelly, noisy — let's be honest, blobs. It's no different from drowning a kitten, and they didn't suffer.'

'You had Sophie for a week!'

'Well, yes. All those nannies and governesses... I thought *that's fine, I'll hardly need to see it*. Then one starts to realise how inhibiting a child will be. Such a tie. Which is why I disposed of the second one as quickly as possible.'

Is she alive after that ordeal?

The charade worked a little too well, Julia suspected.

Bring the cot here. Next to me. Closer!

You should sleep now. You're exhausted.

Plain sailing after that. Lean across. Pillow over face. Then, bliss. Sleep at last! No wonder they found the new mother with a smile on her face...

'Eight years later, the boy comes along, but by the time I convinced his overindulgent father to ease up on the mollycoddling, I discovered the child had evolved a certain amount of character.'

'Last week, did Austin find out? No, no, of course not. Let me guess. The middleman approached you?'

'He said the boy contracted polio, was I supposed to believe that?' Cara's eyes narrowed. 'Once a blackmailer starts, my dear, there's no stopping them, and where does that lead?'

Never overturned a decision, never backed down. Even if it meant Austin publicly admitting his humiliation and destroying his reputation in the process, he would have seen her jailed in a heartbeat.

'Where it leads, Cara, is to killing your husband before he learns his son's still alive, having roped in a stooge to take the fall.'

No one, not even Austin, suspected the mother. The police, the press, even the squad of hard-boiled, heard-it-all, seen-it-all private detectives that Austin hired had been fooled by Cara's tight-lipped grief. A mother of two baby daughters, who'd died in their cribs? They'd swallowed her lies, taken her tears at face value, and never questioned Cara's distress, because it was genuine, all right. Just not caused by grief for the tragic, short lives of her babies, but by the fear of being caught. The constant strain of waiting for that tap on her shoulder...

'You exploited Ezra's loyalty, like you exploited everyone else.'

Julia could picture the scene, Cara wringing her hands, telling him how the kidnappers had contacted her, asking for money. *If I tell anyone — Austin, the police — they'll kill him, they said.* As a book-keeper he'd know that, like all women, she had no funds of her own, *so if you could find your way to misappropriating a few hundred...* Fooled by her crocodile tears, and swayed by her vulnerability, he'd have jumped at the chance. *By the time the theft's discovered, I'll have Thomas home safe. You'll be hailed as a hero!*

For her plan to succeed, of course, the theft did need to be discovered, and that check at the bank wasn't random at all. Cara would have told Austin how she'd heard rumours ... didn't believe them ... but he ought perhaps to confirm all the same ... if only to clear the poor man's name. Either way, Ezra certainly believed it was random. Why else would he be so hurt when Austin sacked him and served notice for eviction as well, yet still refused to explain his actions? While simple, trusting Thora never dreamt Mrs. Forbes would plant a stash of cash in the sideboard when she dropped by on the pretext of visiting their son, then tip off Austin about where to look.

A long time in the planning…

'Finally, you arranged a pretend exchange with the kidnappers, telling Ezra to bring his shotgun along, just in case.'

The poor sod was dead by the time Austin rode up Windmill Hill, where she shot him with both barrels in the back. Did he know it was Cara? Julia doubted it somehow. The bitch was too cowardly to look him in the face, but the sad truth was, Austin died without knowing his son was alive.

For what seemed like eternity, the room was silent, apart from the pendulum ticking away inside the grandfather clock. With a jolt, Julia realised it had stopped raining.

'As I see it,' Cara said eventually, 'we have one of two choices. We can either put this ridiculous conversation behind us and be the friends that we were. Indeed, why don't you come to Venice with me? You have no ties here, just a lowly position —'

'Or?'

'Or, and forgive my bluntness, my dear, but I very much doubt your employer rewards you quite as loyally as you deserve. As of this week, I'm a very rich woman —'

'You're buying my silence?'

'Funding a new life for a dear friend,' Cara corrected. 'On condition, of course, that new life is far, far from here, and that my dear friend doesn't mention this nonsense to another living soul.'

'Suppose the money runs out? Suppose I come back?'

'Suppose you do.' Cara pushed back her shoulders and jutted her chin. 'Who will the police believe? A much-maligned widow and twice bereaved mother, who's behaved with dignity throughout every ordeal? Or a scheming, penniless, blackmailer? The choice is yours, but you should know that I haven't come this far to lose everything at this stage.'

'Are you threatening me?'

'I'm simply saying that I deserve my freedom. I've worked for it, suffered for it, and, let's be clear, Mrs. McAllister, I intend to enjoy every moment, because when it boils down, you don't have a single shred of proof.'

'Ah, well, that's where you're wrong.' Julia swept aside the black *cloisonné* screen. 'Modern technology is a wonderful thing.'

Cara frowned, but not at the contraption on the table. 'I sacked you,' she said archly.

'You did,' said the pockmarked young footman with slightly bucked teeth, whose tails sat too short on his gangly frame when he'd served cakes at Julia's first visit. 'You sacked me because you told everyone I sold gossip to the papers about you, but you gave them that story, not me, and after that, no one'd hire me.'

'They will now,' Julia said brightly. 'You see this, Cara, is a phonograph.' She tapped a mahogany box, not unlike her camera case, on which a gleaming brass horn had been mounted. 'It has recorded every second of our conversation on the wax cylinders your much maligned footman just stuffed in that black Gladstone bag, and whose footsteps you can now hear sprinting down the corridor to where a brougham is waiting to take him to DCI Dudley.'

CHAPTER 34

Sunday afternoon. Sunlight spiked rays of gold through the withering leaves, droplets of water dripped off the trees, and the air smelled earthy and rich.

Julia stared up at the imposing red brickwork, stepped gables and soaring chimney stacks that was Lindale Manor. It wasn't true that every word had been recorded. For one thing, the phonograph could only manage two minutes at a time, and, given the need for silence and stealth, there would have been an equally long gap while the footman changed cylinders. Also, the brougham wasn't waiting to take them to DCI Dudley. In an ideal world, Julia would have sent the recordings to DI John Collingwood, but the world wasn't ideal. The brougham went straight to the chief superintendent.

She stooped to pick a rosebud, perfect and pink in its tightness and innocence, despite the end of the season.

Right now, Cara would be lying, denying, and crying her lovely eyes out, but Blaine wouldn't fall for it twice. He'd moved heaven and earth to find Thomas. He'd feared for him, grieved for him, prayed and despaired for him, it had overshadowed his career and cost him his marriage — and all the while, it was a sham.

The tragedy didn't end there. Thomas might be rich beyond his wildest dreams, but there was no telling how far or how fast the polio would spread, and there was no cure for this pernicious disease. *No place like home, no jam like Forbes*, but no amount of money could keep his young muscles from wasting, or halt the paralysis in his limbs, or stop him dying from respiratory failure. If that wasn't enough, he'd be haunted by the knowledge that his mother traded him on the open market

232

like a horse. Even the couple who'd raised him were now accessory to kidnap. More victims sacrificed on Cara's altar of spite.

But as Julia skirted the ornamental lake, across a lawn that would give a snooker table a run for its money, towards the fortified tower that Henry VIII stayed in, her heart wasn't heavy for them.

It was because this business was not finished yet.

'My brooch?' Lexie's big, blue eyes bulged. 'What does that have to do with anything?'

'It has to do with everything,' Julia said.

They were walking, just the two of them, through botanical gardens strewn with leaves, nuts and twigs brought down in the rain. Unsurprisingly for a woman who was primed to receive visitors at any time, Lexie wore a cornflower blue day dress over the tightest corset this side of the Pennines. And where the colour served to accentuate her eyes, the corset highlighted her breasts, which was the point. Even a stunning swallow set with rose-cut diamonds and a bright ruby eye couldn't outshine that cleavage.

Precious in sentimental, rather than financial terms was how Lexie referred to it. Exactly. Having sold off every antique, every picture, every ring, necklace and pin, what odds the diamonds she flashed around Broadhurst and Oakbourne were fake? Except for one little swallow. A gift from her late husband? Had it belonged to her mother? Who knows, but it made Julia think about the priceless items in Austin's room rubbing shoulders with shepherdess figurines, second-rate silver cufflinks, and cheap clothes brushes.

'Why would a man of Austin's stature keep gewgaws?' Julia said, as they passed under the arch. 'These were the sort of knick-knacks shop girls bought, then I realised. Not shop girls, but girls — women — who earned very little money, yet bought their lover gifts all the same. Sacrifices which obviously touched Austin deeply, smacking of two-sided relationships, not shallow affairs.'

Lexie spun round to face her. 'Are you saying he wouldn't tell me why he ruined us because he was honourable and had given his word?'

'He *was* honourable, Lexie, he *had* given his word, and I'm afraid your father ruined you, not Austin. He was the one who gambled everything away, and in return for your lands, Austin cleared the Davenport debts and swore to never speak of it. That's not what I was driving at, though. It was those very tokens of affection in his display case that set me thinking about other small items, stolen in the dead of night. But more importantly, it got me thinking about Joshua Reynolds.'

The challenge in Lexie's eyes gave way to pain. 'I always knew you were smart.'

'You shouldn't have dragged the others into it, Lexie.'

'I will take full responsibility for my crime, and I will go to my grave denying they had any involvement.' Lexie blew out her cheeks. 'But...! Grace was growing up fast, and since old maids have no value in the marriage market, I thought I might fund the renovations by producing exotic shrubs for local parks, gardens and cemeteries, because the last thing I wanted was to charge an entrance fee. Those poor factory workers suffer so much hardship that they deserve to see these beautiful botanical rooms for free.' She swept her arm around the roses and hydrangeas, the camellias and the dwarf maples, perfect in their individual settings. 'Unfortunately, I was drowning in debt, until Dickon had a brainwave.'

'Exploiting Lydia's artistic skills, photographic memory and intelligence gathered at social events, you knew exactly which paintings to forge.'

'Dickon holds the ladder and keeps watch. Grace slips through the window, parts the pictures from their frames, and swaps the canvas. Dickon then passes the originals to a contact in London, and the proceeds, which are truly pathetic I might add, go straight on renovations.' Lexie leaned forward in a cloud of vanilla, sandalwood and patchouli to grab Julia's hand. 'What gave me away?'

'The fact that your house is varnish from top to bottom, yet Lydia was splattered with multi-coloured oils. And the fact that the last one, the Joshua Reynolds, wasn't quite dry.'

The smudge on Julia's clothes that wouldn't come out.

'Grace and Lydia have nowhere to go, but can you at least give Dickon the chance to run?'

'No.'

By her own admission, Lexie seduced Austin as a means to an end. Why not Dickon, Julia thought? One possibility was that Lexie had manipulated him into believing she was the victim, hence his sudden, dare one say protective, appearance when he thought she was in danger, and the willingness with which he sprang into action against an armed protagonist.

'When you turned up this afternoon, telling me what Cara had done, I thought I'd be thanking you for clearing my name. Instead —' Lexie swallowed. 'Is that vagrant a ... what do they call them, undercover policeman?'

'The answer to that is also *no*.' Julia beckoned Billy over with an energetic wave. 'They call them grass inspectors.'

Lexie's hip-swinging sensuality and inviting cleavage wasn't the product of coercion, any more than Dickon's reaction when faced with a supposed cornered fugitive was one of duty. It was love.

'Or in this case,' Julia added, making introductions, 'your second handyman.'

It wasn't easy, talking him into it. In fact, it was a nightmare. But once the Davenports got past the language barrier, and Billy saw that, this way, he was helping everyone, since his remuneration would be in the form of donations to the Broadhurst Children's hospital, Julia thought they'd fit together rather nicely.

CHAPTER 35

The clouds that had lingered low, grey and heavy over Oakbourne had moved on. Shedding their load over the Chilterns, swelling the chalk streams, drenching the beech woods, and giving life to the seeds. But as the good folk of the town threw open their curtains to admit the Monday morning sun, they noticed an unaccustomed chill in the air. A chill that whispered of change.

A change, not only in swallows gathering in numbers, or the first falling leaves that signalled an end to the long, balmy days of summer. Change from within. The automobile, that ultimate symbol of progress, looked set to replace the horse and carriage on a permanent basis. Locomotives were opening the way for cheap and regular day trips, as well as seaside summer holidays, and the chance to explore foreign lands. The surge in bicycle sales reflected women's rights and independence, because without corsets, hoops and layered skirts that restricted them in every sense, the message was clear. *No longer are we shackled by fashion, by convention or, more importantly, by law. Soon we shall break free of them all.*

With change, though, comes understanding. Sometimes it's seeing life through new eyes. Knowing that you will never again see the victims of crime without seeing possible suspects. And sometimes it's facing what you knew all along, but could not bring yourself to admit...

Julia stood in front of Whitmore Photographic and studied the frontage with an artist's and photographer's eye. She always knew this would be hard...

Collingwood would forgive her for taking the wax cylinders to Blaine. It wasn't his case, and for "him" to have sprung a confession with the aid of a mechanical phonograph, "his" crime scene photographer and a not-so-perfidious footman would have been to rub the chief superintendent's nose in the dirt so deep that even Australia wouldn't be the end of the line. This way, with Blaine feted a hero in what had already made international news, his job, along with Boot Street and Charlie Kincaid, would be safe.

What he wouldn't forgive was being stabbed in the back.

The breaking of trust is the worst of betrayals, if he found out that his cat burglar was actually a master forger as well, and that Julia was complicit in letting them continue, charging her with aiding and abetting was only the start. Even though she'd persuaded Lexie to stop filching the jewels (that was completely reprehensible), promise or no promise, Collingwood wouldn't hesitate to dig up her past.

With tears in her eyes, Julia nailed the sign to the door. Ever since Sam died, she knew she'd have to make this decision. Stay and be lonely. Or start a new life where she didn't have to look over her shoulder. She stepped back to make sure the sign was straight.

SHOOT THE KIDS
HANG THE FAMILY
FRAME THEM ALL

'Now for God's sake,' she told herself sternly, 'stop buggering about and go sign some new models.'

A NOTE TO THE READER

Well, Reader —

If you enjoyed *Bad Blood* — and for heaven's sake why wouldn't you? — I'd very much value your review on **Amazon** and **Goodreads**. And to find out more about what I'm working on next, I'd love for you to join me on **Facebook (Marilyn Todd – Crime Writer)** and **Twitter (@marilyntodd12)**.

Marilyn Todd.

www.marilyntodd.com

Sapere Books is an exciting new publisher of brilliant fiction and popular history.

To find out more about our latest releases and our monthly bargain books visit our website: **saperebooks.com**

Printed in Great Britain
by Amazon